"Let go of me," she whispered.

Her eyes stared into his. The granite had changed to hazel, and as she watched, his eyes turned dark and she forgot to breathe.

"Tomorrow? You're going tomorrow?" she asked, although it was not her voice at all.

"Tomorrow," he echoed as her lips parted unconsciously. "Or now," he growled as he moved closer, his eyes on her lips, on the soft smoothness of her long neck, the trembling at the base of her throat. "If you want me to go, you'd better decide. Now."

She managed to say shakily, "Now would be better. Go now." Far better. This was dangerous, playing with explosive unknowns. She ached for his touch, but she had to say no. Even though she trembled for him....

VANESSA GRANT started writing her first romance at the age of twelve and hasn't forgotten the excitement of having a love story come to life on paper. After spending four years refitting the forty-six-foot yacht they live on, she and her husband, Brian, and their teenage son set sail south to Mexico along the North American West Coast. Vanessa divides her time between her writing, sailing and exploring the harbors of the Pacific Coast. She often writes her love stories on her portable computer while anchored in remote inlets. Vanessa says, "I believe in love and in happy endings."

Books by Vanessa Grant

HARLEQUIN PRESENTS
1209—STRANDED HEART
1234—AWAKENING DREAMS
1264—WILD PASSAGE
1289—TAKING CHANCES
1322—SO MUCH FOR DREAMS
1386—ONE SECRET TOO MANY

HARLEQUIN ROMANCE
2888—THE CHAUVINIST

VANESSA GRANT

the touch of love

Harlequin Books

TORONTO • NEW YORK • LONDON
AMSTERDAM • PARIS • SYDNEY • HAMBURG
STOCKHOLM • ATHENS • TOKYO • MILAN

This book is dedicated to
Jill and Nigel of *Magic Tern,*
companions on the voyage north

Harlequin Presents first edition January 1992
ISBN 0-373-11426-5

Original hardcover edition published in 1990
by Mills & Boon Limited

THE TOUCH OF LOVE

CHAPTER ONE

BY THE time he got to Queen Charlotte City, Scott thoroughly regretted his decision to take the ferry. He could have flown. He realised by now that he *should* have taken the jet from Vancouver to the Queen Charlotte Islands.

Instead, he had taken one ferry to Vancouver Island and another to Queen Charlotte, thinking that it would be better for the baby.

That was before he discovered that Robin Scott Alexander was subject to violent attacks of seasickness. Incredible that he and this baby could share blood, yet take to the sea so differently.

Sitting in the aft passenger lounge of the ferry, Scott crooned at the baby. Robin Scott howled back at him. Scott made rocking motions with his arms in hopes of enticing the unhappy infant into silence, perhaps even into sleep. During all his own years at sea, Scott had secretly believed that seasickness was psychological, a physical symptom of fear. Yet here he was, saddled with a two-month-old bundle of screaming, whimpering agonies, and a twenty-six-hour ferry trip. Psychological? He had always tried to be patient with his seasick crew members, but he vowed to be more sympathetic in future.

'Easy, kiddo,' he crooned, shifting the baby up to his shoulder.

Behind him, an irritable voice muttered, 'Shut that bloody kid up, for God's sake! I'm getting sick of this!'

So was he! Scott stood up with Robin in his arms and grimaced wryly at the amused stare of the matronly woman sitting opposite. Earlier, Scott had nursed the futile hope that she might offer to hold the baby, might silence Robin with some magical motherly touch. Unfortunately, his wishful thinking had been pure fantasy. The matron had smiled sympathetically, but had shown no sign of wanting to take over Scott's problem.

Walking, pacing between the rows of passenger seats on the *Queen of the North*, Scott finally soothed the infant into stillness. Silence, then the faint moaning, then the stiffening of the little body. He recognised the warning signs, knew he had only seconds to avert disaster. He dodged around two slow-moving, elderly men and dashed through the cafeteria, around three businessmen and a young mother with a toddler. He ran desperately for the men's room and—this time—got there before young Robin threw up all over yet another clean shirt!

A day and a night on the ferry and Scott had worked his way through three shirts and two pairs of trousers. And this was supposed to be simpler than taking the jet?

But it had seemed such a good idea. Robin Scott Alexander had been an angel back in Vancouver. Too young to realise he had lost his mother, to worry that his future was very uncertain, the baby had slept through the funeral, and had gurgled happily in his crib while Scott sorted through Donna's possessions, crating up the personal things that the baby might want some day, sending them on by courier to his own home on Cortes Island. Sorting, throwing out, saving, he had learned more about Donna than he had known during her short life.

While he sorted through the souvenirs of Donna's life, he had wrestled with the problem of this baby, Donna's child by a man she had never been willing to name. He did not want to leave the child to the whims of the social welfare system, orphaned and alone, and yet——

Then he had found the letters, just as Robin opened his throat and let out a mighty wail. A new nappy—thank the lord for the public health nurse who had come and shown Scott about nappies and formulas! Then a bottle, and, with Robin sucking contentedly on it, Scott had read the letters that gave him the answer to little Robin's future. One phone call and he was sure baby Robin's father would be flying to Vancouver to take charge of his son.

The Queen Charlotte Islands, those ancient bits of land in the cold Pacific waters of northern British Columbia. Scott had seen the hills and mountains from the decks of various ships over the years. Always passing by, he had never set foot on their shores. His memory held scraps of information gathered from magazine articles and film documentaries; an impression of ancient forests, of quiet, good-hearted people, a world apart from the rat race.

A good omen, he had thought. A home for young Robin amid the sounds of sea birds and the love of people close to nature.

Robin. Donna had named the baby after its father.

But there was no telephone number to match the name on Donna's letters. There could be any number of reasons for that. The man might have his number under a business listing. How the devil had Donna, a pure city girl, met a man from those remote islands? Scott had frowned down at the baby, staring into dark eyes that seemed black in most lights. A stranger, this baby, with dark hair and dark eyes, with none of the fair colouring of the Alexanders. Although young Robin Scott Alexander had never been exposed to the hot sun, his skin was darker than Scott's own weathered fair skin,

and was certainly unlike Donna's smooth, pale flesh.
Perhaps the father was Haida Indian, or part Haida. It
was certainly a possibility, if he lived on the Charlottes.

Reading the letters Donna left behind, he had realised
guiltily that he had been too busy with his own life, that
Donna had needed him and he had not been there for
her. And now little Robin needed someone. Scott
frowned, realising he was planning to hand the infant
over to a name on a piece of paper.

What other choice was there? Sylvia, Donna's foster-
mother, was too frail to take on a child, and there was
no one else. Caroline would be shocked if he suggested
she look after this child, and rightly so. He shied away
from the idea of asking Caroline to marry him and give
Robin Scott a home and a family. Marriage had never
had a place in Scott's plans for the future.

No. It was impossible for him to give the baby a home.
A man could not look after a child by remote control
from a ship in the Beaufort Sea, even if his year's work
was usually completed in the eighteen weeks or so when
those northern waters were navigable.

So the answer was in Queen Charlotte City, a mere
hour by commercial jet from Vancouver. He had rejected the idea of the jet, not wanting to disembark at
Sandspit airport with an infant, dependent on local
transportation to get him across the harbour from
Sandspit to Queen Charlotte, to find an address that was
only a number on a piece of paper. He disliked the idea
of being ejected from a taxi, complete with baby and
nappy bag, to confront a stranger, yet knew he could
not dump little Robin in a hotel room while he checked
things out.

He might be able to rent a car at the airport, but he
had been in enough small northern communities to know
that he could easily end up stranded at the airport with

a telephone number for a car-rental outfit, and no one answering at the other end. Far better to arrive with his own transport. After all, the *Queen of the North* made regular trips to the Queen Charlotte Islands. A big, modern roll-on roll-off ferry with state-rooms and dining-rooms. Better, travelling with a baby on the ferry, driving off in his own truck. Especially as Robin was such a placid little thing. The baby would sleep the voyage away.

In fact, Robin did sleep, all the way from Port Hardy across the Queen Charlotte Sound, to Bella Bella and across Milbanke Sound. Throughout the journey, Scott stayed at the baby's side, chained by his unaccustomed role as nursemaid.

Normally, Scott would have looked up acquaintances among the crew. He had caught a glimpse of the captain, had recognised him, and would have liked to make his way up to the bridge and share reminiscences of their days as seamen on the coastguard's *Alexander MacKenzie*. Instead, he had stayed with Robin, appreciating for the first time how much a child could trap a young mother.

Then, in the middle of the night in Princess Royal Channel, the south-easterly winds had hit. Nothing dangerous, nothing he would have thought about twice, but enough to upset passengers with frail stomachs.

And Donna's baby.

When Scott went into the men's room to rinse out his first shirt, all he could see was the soles of shoes through the spaces below the cubicle doors. Sick passengers. Sick baby.

Robin alternated between screaming and throwing up all through the night, falling into a fitful sleep as the ship docked in Prince Rupert. Then, at noon, when they set sail again, Robin whimpered. They crossed Chatham Sound, windy but not terribly rough, and Robin writhed in Scott's arms. They cleared the islands into Hecate Strait, and the baby gave up any pretence of calm.

Queen of the North, big and sturdy though she was, shuddered as she crashed down on the steep waves of the Hecate Strait. A southeaster, with all the anger of the Pacific flooding into the big, shallow strait. The waves were steep and violent. Miserable going in the most seaworthy of vessels.

After changing out of his third shirt, even Scott couldn't face the thought of supper in the cafeteria, and in fact the kitchen had closed. Scott got himself hot chocolate from a dispenser, then took one of Robin's bottles down to have it warmed. Robin rejected the bottle in any case, and Scott didn't finish his chocolate.

They cleared the markers at Lawn Point and turned to make the run into Queen Charlotte harbour. Sheltered from the south wind by the mass of Moresby Island, the *Queen* settled into calm water.

Robin fell asleep just as the announcement came on the loud speakers. All passengers to the car decks.

The matronly woman from the passenger lounge stopped Scott as he started down the stairs to deck C. 'Next time,' she advised in husky, expert tones, 'give the poor thing a bit of Gravol before you take him on to a boat. He shouldn't have to be so sick. A bit of Gravol and he'd sleep the whole trip away.'

'Thanks,' he muttered, knowing there would be no next time. His custody of this child was purely temporary.

She bent to look at the baby, stroking his cheek with a gentle finger. Robin opened dark eyes and stared at her without expression and the woman looked from the baby to the man holding him. 'Takes after his mother, doesn't he?' she decided. 'He certainly doesn't look much like you.'

* * *

Melody tried the amateur radio on Sunday night, but conditions were bad. She could hardly hear the Vancouver net control, much less the Pacific ship stations. Nevertheless, she gave her call-sign.

'Go ahead, Mel,' net control replied. 'Call your station.'

She called Robin's high seas call-sign.

'He's answering you,' said net control. 'Do you copy him?'

'Nothing at all. I've got a lot of interference here.'

She heard net control informing Robin, 'She's got QRM. Try again.'

Robin called again, but she could hear only the distorted Spanish of a Mexican station riding in on sky wave. So she sent a brief, impersonal message to Robin via net control, and he passed back his position and his weather. Ten-knot winds. Clear skies. Everything's fine.

Amateur radio was too public for private messages, but she was glad to know that he was still out there, that if he had problems, they were too small for him to mention.

She signed off and threw the power switch on the noisy radio, then plotted the new longitude and latitude on her map of the Pacific Ocean. She stuck in one more pin, this one with a little red button on its head. If Robin wanted to get away from it all, he was surely succeeding. There was no land within six hundred miles of that pin.

She went for a moonlit walk, looking out over the harbour from her hillside vantage point. Earlier, she had seen the ferry coming in, had known that tomorrow there would be milk in the grocery store again. Thursday's ferry had not arrived due to bad weather, so the island residents hadn't had fresh milk in the stores for five days.

A cloud slid over the moon, throwing darkness around her. Below, lights streaked across the harbour. A gusty wind twisted down the hill where Melody stood. She shivered in her thick jacket. It was cold for April, fresh sea air on the wind.

She turned to go back home, clear-headed now, ready to work. She locked the front door as she closed it behind herself, discarded her shoes and went around locking up the rest of the house for the night. Then she went upstairs to the sound-room Jeff had helped her build.

Tonight she closed the soundproof shutters on the dormer window. She was going to record and she needed to shut out the sounds of the wind and the night. And old Mr Edgley, who lived across the creek, complained when she polluted the air with music after nine at night.

She turned up the thermostat against the chill, although she would rather have lit a fire in the fireplace. She loved the warm crackling of flames licking on dried wood, but the noise would contaminate her recording.

For a moment she felt her own solitude, had an unaccustomed image of herself as a woman alone in an old wooden house on an empty hillside. Empty life filled with only the fantasies of music. It was an unpleasant image, not true, but it was the cruel vision Peter Hammond would have had if he could see her.

With the soundproofing shutting her away from the world, and the synthesiser turned on, she forgot time. She forgot Peter, who no longer had any rights over her mind. She forgot Robin in his little ship on the big ocean. She forgot everything but the music that possessed her.

CHAPTER TWO

MELODY woke on Monday morning at eight-thirty, later than usual, thick-headed and yearning to curl back up under the covers after her late night. She resisted the lazy impulse. Seven of the recordings were complete, ready for Robin and the band, but there were five more, ideas roughed out but not ready yet, and the recording studio was booked in Los Angeles for a date only six weeks away.

She got up and pulled on her housecoat, more for warmth than for modesty. She usually slept in an over-sized T-shirt. With the trees surrounding her house, the chances of anyone looking in on her were minimal. She was accustomed to wandering around the house in bare feet and the T-shirt most mornings until she had consumed at least three cups of coffee.

Not today, though. That wind was cold, and somehow the electric heating system was not keeping up with the cool wind. She went around turning up the thermostats in all the rooms, cursing Amanda and Charlie for their nineteen-year-old decision to pull out the oil furnace and install electric heating. It might have made sense back then, when electricity was so much cheaper, but now...

Of course, Amanda and Charlie had hardly ever been here to realise how much better the oil furnace would have been. There would have been something so much more *warm* about heated air blasting out of vents in the floor, but from their long-term hotel room in the Caribbean they could hardly be expected to think about the virtues of cuddly warmth. It was just lucky that they had left the fireplaces intact!

She put on the coffee to drip, then took the recording she had made last night into the living-room and pushed it into the stereo.

The living-room was massive, a long room running from the front of the house to the back. It was divided into two parts, more by decor than by shape. The front, with windows looking out over the front lawn, through the trees to the water, was the public part, decorated with light, old-style wallpaper and big oak beams. There were two big over-stuffed sofas, the television set, bookshelves and coffee-tables, and a massive picture window.

The back was private, the walls dark walnut, the curtains a deep, rust-coloured brocade. Everything was warm and dark and private, even the two big easy chairs that faced away from the public part, looking out at shadowed moss under old, twisted trees, at the creek that murmured as it moved endlessly, dividing the Connacher property from the Edgley property.

The stereo system was at the back, positioned by Charlie for optimum listening from those two chairs. Typical Connacher priorities: music came first. Melody had installed the new ham radio transceiver there, too, mainly because it was close to the antenna tower she and Robin had put up years ago, when they had jointly gained their amateur radio certificates.

Her eyes fell on the radio transceiver and she smiled, thinking that Charlie would have a fit when he found out how she had contaminated his favourite room with the dits and dahs of Morse code, the howling and squealing of distorted radio signals. Certainly that had never been Charlie's intention when he and Amanda had bought this hideaway. But, possession being nine points of the law, Melody was the one in control here, no matter how the deed of title was worded. And Charlie might rant and rave, but in the end he would let her have her way. Years ago, after one disastrous attempt to put her on stage, Charlie had learned it was easier to give in to his daughter than to fight her.

Before turning the stereo on, she went to get a cup of freshly brewed coffee, then curled her feet up under her in the big chair nearest the window and reached one hand out to push the button that would start the music.

She listened with her dark eyes closed, her hands with their short, unpolished nails curled around the warmth of her coffee mug, her unbrushed brunette hair tumbled wildly around her head. The bass guitar took over the room, then the percussion instruments, then Melody's own voice, which was only a substitute to put the words in place over the music. It would be Robin singing the words in the studio, and in addition to this version she would give the band the written music and words, and a clean recording with only instrumentation, no voice. In fact, if Robin turned up in Queen Charlotte in time, she would get him to do the voice-over.

It was good, with the dreamy, poetic rhythm that she was best at. Her mind substituted Robin's deep, powerful voice for her own and she felt the excitement growing. This one was going to be winner. It might be the title song for the album.

The music faded to silence with a final, emotional chord from the bass guitar. All synthetic, the guitar and the percussion instruments, but Jeff had advised her well. The equipment upstairs could have lain in one of the best recording studios in North America, and no one listening could have told that this was not real musicians playing tunes to Melody's command.

She shut off the stereo and went for another cup of coffee, deciding against breakfast because she was out of yoghurt and had no milk to pour over her muesli. She would buy milk today, after her session upstairs and before she went to the radio station. She wrote herself a note—'milk'—and tacked it up on her bulletin board.

She washed up her supper dishes from last night as she drank the coffee, her mind already upstairs in the sound-room, then she poured another cup of coffee and carried it with her upstairs to her bedroom.

The doorbell rang just as she pulled the sweater out of its drawer. She hesitated, then started unzipping her robe. She would dress first. Nine o'clock on a Monday morning. Surely no one would be in such a massive hurry that they couldn't wait while she put on her clothes.

She shrugged out of the robe just as the buzzer went again. Damn! This was the islands and surely nothing was that urgent? It was probably the postman with the contracts from her agent. Peter always sent them by registered post, which she could never see the point of because it was no faster and they could easily be re-copied and sent again if they should go astray. Registered meant that she had to come to the door and sign for the envelope, inevitably meaning that she had to interrupt a session in the music-room, throwing everything out of sync and putting her back a half-hour by the time she got back to work and in the mood after listening to the postman's gossip. Melody knew her weaknesses. She was too easily distracted. Two or three small interruptions could throw her whole morning into a useless frustration. So she locked her door when she went to the music-room, turned the unlisted telephone off, and everyone knew that you didn't try to contact Melody Connacher before one in the afternoon.

She should be thankful that she was behind schedule this morning, that the postman would only interrupt her dressing, not her creative mood. She zipped the dressing-gown back up and went downstairs to the door, throwing it open.

'In a hurry this morning?' she asked mildly, her anger toned down to friendly criticism. Her temper flared quickly, but anger never lasted long for Melody.

The man in front of her was a total stranger.

Melody pushed her hair back in an unconscious attempt to tidy herself and look less like a sleepy slob. She said briskly, 'Yes. Can I help you?'

It was not the postman, not unless Canada Post had given up on blue uniforms and gone to immaculate grey trousers and leather, sheepskin-lined jackets. Not to mention the captain's hat that topped it all off, giving him the look of an inappropriately polished but tough man of the sea.

She started to smile, then the curve of her lips faded to a frown as she realised that his hazel eyes had no warm lights in them, his mouth no friendly curve to it. It was character in his face, she decided, not handsomeness. She felt a sensual jolt that surprised her, even while she decided thankfully that he was a stranger whose frown was not going to mean trouble for her.

'Is Robin Connacher here?' His voice was firm, pleasant, and he was accustomed to people jumping when he spoke. Behind him, she could see the black truck he must have driven up her twisted driveway. It was a four-wheel drive, shining and expensive. Like the man, it was obvious that the truck meant business.

'Sorry,' she said, smiling slightly, her mind putting musical notes to words about a sea-captain with a big truck and tired laughter-lines radiating from his eyes. He was obviously an islander, although she knew she had never seen him before. She would have remembered. He had the tough confidence that went with the wild north. A fisherman perhaps, maybe even a neighbour. The house down the hill had been for sale for six months now, and last week the estate agent's car had been there—he must have been showing someone around. There was no laughter in this man's voice or his eyes, though, so Melody snapped out of her whimsical daze and repeated more firmly, 'Sorry, he's not here.'

'He doesn't live here?' The voice seemed to lose something of its authority. 'This isn't Robin Connacher's house?'

'You've got the right place.' Did Robin live here? Did Robin actually *live* anywhere specific? She shrugged that question away and said, 'But you can't see him. Sorry. If you'll give me a message for him, I can see it gets delivered.'

'That won't do.' He was frowning.

She resisted an urge to salute and say, Aye, aye, Captain.

'I've got to talk to him.' He looked back at his truck and she followed his gaze, then stared at him when he grumbled, 'Did you ever think of getting someone in to fix up that driveway?'

'With four-wheel drive, I wouldn't think you'd have a problem,' she snapped back. 'My van does it all the time.'

He shrugged something away. Then the irritation was gone and he was smiling down at her. He wasn't a tall man, but then neither was she tall, and he had the big, heavy shoulders of a wrestler or a weight-lifter. She felt small and ridiculously feminine.

He said, 'I'm a bit over-tired. I took the ferry up from Port Hardy and didn't have a very good sleep in my hotel last night.'

She nodded and tried to pretend that she did not realise his eyes had fixed on the free swelling of her breasts under the soft housecoat. It was time he left, past time she got to work. She could spend the morning on her front veranda, feeling tousled and oddly vulnerable, or she could work on the eighth song.

'Look, do you have a message for Robin, or——?'

He shook his head, pushing his hands into the pockets of the leather jacket. 'No, I have to see him personally. I take it he's at work? When will he be home? I could come back this evening or——'

'He won't be here.' She heard a sound, muffled, like a baby's cry, and he jerked around towards his truck. She said, 'It's probably a raven. They're all over the islands.' He must not be an islander, not when he talked about staying in a hotel. She added, 'They're fantastic mimics. The ravens, I mean. They can sound like a baby, or a dune-buggy engine, or a rock dropping in water.'

His eyes flew from his truck back to her. The sound came again before she realised that she was wrong, that it was no raven. He looked uneasy, something she suspected did not happen all that often. 'It's a baby,' he said.

She laughed. 'Your day to look after the baby?' He was obviously not accustomed to the job.

The baby yelped again and he jerked, torn between going to the truck and not going. 'No,' he said abruptly. 'I—oh, hell! Just wait a minute, would you?'

He ran to the truck just as the cries turned to wails. He was back with the baby in his arms, holding it as if he had done it a lot, but still with that uneasy look in his eyes. The baby didn't stop crying, although he joggled it gently and rubbed its back.

'Maybe it needs changing,' she suggested. 'Or feeding?'

'Maybe,' he agreed. 'Listen, I really have to see Robin Connacher. I'm Scott Alexander, and I've come up here from the lower mainland specially to see him.'

She shook her head. 'I'm sorry, but you're out of luck. He's not here. As I said, I can get a message to him, but unless you want to sit around a few weeks waiting, you won't get to see him here.'

'Damn!' The baby's wailing gained power with the man's curse. He lowered his voice, pressing the baby against his shoulder and saying with a subdued anger, 'It's urgent that I see him. Wherever he is, I've got to get there and talk to him. I—— Who are you?'

She frowned, wondering just what Robin was involved in. Wild though he was, it really wasn't like her twin to get into the kind of trouble that brought tough-looking men to his door. If this tough stranger had come looking for Charlie, she could have believed it more easily. Her father was always in scrapes. But Robin?

'I'm Melody Connacher,' she said, suddenly wondering why he had a baby with him. A baby, and he was a stranger, staying in a hotel, so he had no family locally. Of course, he might have a wife with him, but in that case, why wasn't she in the truck, holding the baby? Where was the baby's mother? And what on earth was *he* doing here?

Realising that she should have been suspicious from the first, she demanded abruptly, 'What is it you want with Robin?'

'Where is he?' he countered, speaking softly so as not to disturb the baby's sudden silence.

'Away,' she snapped. She could feel her heart pounding. It would be hours after he left before she could get herself quieted and in a mood for working. Damn the man! 'Why do you want him?'

'It's personal.' The baby stirred. The man sighed in a way that made her remember that he had said he was tired. She almost invited him into the house, but she knew better than that. He could be anyone at all. An axe murderer. A baby kidnapper.

He demanded, 'Are you Connacher's wife?'

'Robin's not——' She broke off, knowing she should not give out personal details about Robin. Then, not realising she was going to tell him, she said abruptly, 'I'm his sister.'

'He's not married?'

She crossed her arms over her breasts and the man nodded, as if she had answered his question. 'You must have a phone number for him. Or an address, a hotel where he is at the moment. It's really very important.'

He was persuasive, his voice sending messages that said he was trustworthy and responsible and she could tell him anything. But her childhood and those two years in Los Angeles had given her a wariness that reminded her that Robin was famous enough to be fair game for all kinds of crazy schemes. 'No,' she said. 'I can give him a message if you like. Then if he wants to see you, he'll call you. I don't give out his phone number or his address.' She smothered a grin at that, thinking of city things like telephones, and Robin on his little ship in the middle of the Pacific Ocean.

The baby drowned out his answer with a powerful scream. Melody winced. The man holding the infant shouted to drown out the howling. 'Look, Ms Connacher, we've got to talk! But first of all this baby needs tending to!'

The wind twisted over the veranda and she hugged herself closer, aware of her bare feet as his eyes dropped to the hem of her housecoat. She snapped, 'It's not *my* baby.'

He scowled at her, the expression in his eyes as violent as his arms were tender on the child. The poor baby howled even more loudly. 'He needs changing, but it's bloody cold out here. Why don't you open that door and let us in. We can talk better inside.'

'No.' They glared at each other. A baby could be a novel gimmick to get into a strange house. It was not his house, but Melody felt nervous. Not that she thought he would physically force his way inside, but those eyes had changed from hazel to granite and he was the kind of man who got his way regardless of rules or opponents. She bit her lip and asked again, 'What is it you want Robin for?'

'Not me, it's the baby that wants him.'

'The baby?' she repeated, her voice sharp and startled.

'Yes. His baby.'

'His——' Her lips were open and nothing was coming out. Robin's baby? The baby *did* have Robin's glowing skin, his dark hair, a heritage from an unidentified Latin ancestor. Even the eyes. But—— 'You can't just burst in here and——'

'I'm not *in* anywhere,' he corrected wryly. She felt his presence like a physical blow as he shifted a few inches closer. 'I'm out in the cold.'

She shook her head, sending the curls tumbling as she finished in a rising voice '——and claim a strange baby is my brother's. You—you think just because he looks like Robin that you can——'

'Does he?' He looked down at the baby, his own eyes hazel again, assessing, as he said, 'I thought he must. He certainly doesn't look like Donna.'

Donna? She had never even *heard* Robin mention the name Donna! Surely Robin would have told her? Granted, they'd seen little of each other these last two years, but surely he would have told her if he'd fathered a child? This had to be a con, although this stranger looked far too blunt and direct for a con man. She bit her lip, unable to keep her eyes off the baby with Robin's eyes, her eyes. She said, 'I don't know anyone named Donna.'

'Can't we leave that until later?' His voice had lost the aggressiveness, but this firm, persuasive gentleness might be every bit as dangerous as the lord-high-captain voice. She started to tell him it was not her baby, that she had no reason to believe it was Robin's either, but before the words could come he seemed to read her mind.

He said, 'It's not *my* baby either, but it is crying, and shouldn't we look after its problems before we settle our own? A new nappy and a bottle of formula.'

'I don't have any nappies. You'll have to go down to the Shop Easy, or——' Suddenly she found herself with an armful of squalling baby. She clutched instinctively, afraid of dropping the infant. 'Listen, Mr Whoever-you-are, I don't know anything about looking after babies! You can't just dump it here and——'

'I'm getting the nappies,' he said, and he was gone, covering the ground between the veranda and his truck with quick strides. She stood in the doorway while the baby burped something up on her housecoat. She stared after the man, wondering if he really was getting nappies. It was more likely that he would get behind the wheel and drive away.

She shouted, 'If you drive off, I'm calling the police. They'll be here before you can back down to the road!'

He reached into the truck, then emerged with a bag that looked identical to those used by the young mothers around Queen Charlotte. It seemed very out of place in the hands of this muscular he-man type. He was grinning as he slammed the door of the truck and took the stairs up to the veranda towards her two at a time. 'Don't worry, I'm not deserting you. Nappies, as promised, and I believe you about the police. That driveway certainly wasn't made for quick getaways.'

He stopped, close enough that she could smell the soap he had showered with that morning. Fresh and tangy and masculine. She frowned. Her thoughts ran like a soap advertisement, and that should be a warning to her. If she didn't get to work soon, she would be doing advertising copy instead of songs.

He shifted the strap of the bag on to one shoulder and reached the other hand up. She jerked, thinking he was going to touch her, but his fingers brushed the baby's cheek, not Melody's. The infant turned his head towards the man's hand, opening his mouth and sucking noisily on a brown, callused finger. Watching, Melody saw the man's expression change to tenderness as he looked down at the suckling baby. She felt an impulse to reach up and trace the lines drawn on his weathered cheek by that half-smile.

'Are you going to let us in?' he asked, smiling widely enough for her to see laughter-lines crinkle around his eyes. He must have been psychic because he added, 'We're not dangerous.'

'Maybe not the baby,' she said, and his laughter sounded as she had imagined it would, full and real, not forced at all. She stepped back and he was inside before she had time to wonder if she was crazy.

He stopped inside the door, reaching back to close it behind her. She stopped too, waiting.

'Somewhere to change the baby?' he suggested.

She looked towards the living-room and he smiled, his eyes taking in its comfortable elegance. 'The kitchen table?' he suggested. 'That would be better. And we could start warming up a bottle.'

'We?' She looked down and found those eyes staring back at her. Her eyes. Robin's. The eyes they had inherited from their mother. The eyes this baby had inherited from his father? Perhaps. She knew she was not going to turn out the man and this baby, not just yet.

He said firmly, 'Yes, we. Until we get to this baby's father, you and I are the nearest thing it has to kin.'

'His mother? What about the mother?' Surely the mother had not pushed her child aside? 'Robin would never be interested in the kind of woman who——'

'She's dead.' He said it flatly, without emotion, but she stared at him. 'The kitchen,' he reminded her, and she wondered if he was as untouched as he appeared. What had the mother been to him? Kin? She stared at the baby and thought about the kind of odd, inter-twined relationships that seemed to belong in the madness that was LA and the world she had escaped.

The baby shifted and Melody could feel the dampness. First things first. She led the way, still holding the baby because he wasn't offering to. She stopped at the kitchen table and said firmly, 'You'll have to do this. I haven't a clue what to do.'

'You've never changed a baby?'

'Never,' she said firmly.

'Just my luck. I thought all girls baby-sat. Surely——?'

'I didn't have that kind of a childhood.' Now, why had she said that? As if she was inviting his interest! She saw the curiosity, the response that seemed to mean he was as aware of her as she was of him. She had never felt a response to a man's *smell* before. But her nostrils caught that after-shower scent again and she felt an answering quivering deep inside herself. 'Take it,' she said, holding the baby out, rejecting the crazy feelings.

His lips twitched, but he did not quite smile. He took the baby. 'Have you got a bath towel?' She went and got one and he nodded to the table. She spread it out, then watched as he efficiently stripped the lower half of the baby, put the nappy in a plastic bag and said, 'You'll have somewhere to dispose of that?'

'Yes,' she agreed, taking it. She was unable to resist adding, 'You, on the other hand, seem to be an expert in this baby business. Maybe you baby-sat for spending money when you were a kid?'

'No,' he said absently. 'I fished. Put a pot of water on the stove to heat up a bottle.'

A fisherman. She had been right. 'Aye, aye, Captain.' His head jerked around and she grinned. 'You're bossy, you know. You're used to giving orders.'

But she put the water on, although he was the one who fed the baby. 'Somewhere more comfortable?' she suggested, and he followed her into the living-room with baby and bottle. She wanted to sit across from him and watch, intrigued by the sight of the big man holding the tiny baby with such care, fascinated by the look on his face when he bent to watch the tiny person suckling on the rubber nipple.

Perhaps because she wanted so much to watch, and because the desire was uncomfortably stirring, she stood up and said abruptly, 'I have things to do. Make yourself comfortable. I'll be back in a few minutes.'

It was past time she got dressed. She ran up the stairs, leaving him behind.

Her sweater was lying on the bed, her jeans a jumble on the floor where she had dropped them when she picked up her dressing-gown to put it back on. She caught a glimpse of herself in the mirror as she shed the dressing-gown again.

She was tumbled, rumpled, as if she had just come from her bed. She had not yet brushed her hair into tame order this morning. Her lips, always red, looked fuller than usual, vulnerable. No wonder he had stared at her as she told him she was leaving him alone with the baby. She looked ... sensual, she thought, not liking the word.

She dressed quickly, zipped her jeans up and pulled the sweater on. She brushed her hair briskly, taming her curls into waves. When she put the brush down, her hair had its daytime look, smooth and controlled as if she had just been to the salon. A pity, Amanda had always said, that Melody had the dramatic colouring, the full dark lips and the wonderfully wavy hair, when she was the one Connacher who hated to be up on the stage. Wasted.

She made her bed, pulling the blue pile spread smooth. She hung up her robe and put away her T-shirt. She pulled the bedroom door tight behind her and went down the corridor to the music-room, stopping at the head of the stairs and listening, hearing a faint murmur that might be her uninvited guest talking to a baby.

She moved from the synthesiser to the multi-track recorder in her sound-room, her hands hovering, but touching nothing. It was ridiculous to pretend she could work right now. She lifted the page of notes for a hauntingly sad song about a girl at the side of the sea, and her fisherman lover who went out on the herring fishery and lost everything in a cold, fierce winter storm. His life. His love.

She knew that when she went back to the song, the fisherman lover would have changed, taken on a reality that was beyond her usual fantasies. He was downstairs.

She was stalling and she knew it. Avoiding going back, avoiding the complication of this baby and the man. She had learned to protect herself from distractions, to shield herself from the rat race that destroyed what was creative in her, from the trivial tasks that sucked away her spontaneity. Not selfish so much as necessary, because she had almost lost herself before she learned to say no to the people who demanded parts of her.

'You're giving away your power,' Jeff had warned her three years ago. 'You're letting Peter and Robin and all the others have the energy you need, suck your talent dry. You think you owe them something, that you have to give because they ask, but you don't. You owe yourself something. Turn us off. Say no. Find yourself again.'

It had been difficult to say no to Peter. He was more than her agent. At first she had been flattered because he was good-looking and important and he seemed to admire her. She had wanted to be swept off her feet, in love, and he said he loved her. She supposed she had wanted to belong to someone who was actually *there* when she opened her eyes, not flying from Paris to Toronto to the Caribbean. She wanted love, and she had said *yes* when he'd asked her to marry him.

He had moulded her in the image he'd wanted, but she had almost lost herself in the process. She hated the publicity he had said was essential to her career, but when she had said so, his voice had turned from loving tolerance to a sharp weapon. So she had given in to him, but her songs had dried up and she had cried often without knowing why. She had wondered who she was and why she was and what it meant when Peter said he loved her, whether she really loved him.

That was when she had gone to Jeff, the sound man on Robin's band and a good friend. She had been desperate for advice, had known Jeff would see things more clearly than she could.

That horrible scene when she had walked out on Peter seemed unreal now, three years later. She thought it must be unreal to Peter as well. Peter was only her agent now, a good agent and a cool friend. Impossible to think that she had once believed she loved him.

Even Robin had been taking advantage of her in those days, holding her in the rat race of LA when she'd needed to be alone, insisting he needed her at his rehearsals. The day she had told him she was leaving, leaving Peter and LA and going to live in the house at Queen Charlotte, Robin had looked at her as if she had betrayed the bond they had shared from the moment of birth.

She had needed to put over a thousand miles between herself and the world of recording studios and high-pressure productivity, but she had her life the way she wanted it now. She had learned to say no. Most of the time, at least. But saying no to a baby? Robin's baby?

A part of her wanted to push the man back out of the door, to deny that this had anything to do with her. Another part remembered childhood, and backstage rooms, and Robin being there when Amanda and Charlie and everyone else forgot. Robin's child downstairs. If it was, it would be the closest thing to a child of her own that was ever likely to be.

CHAPTER THREE

THE baby was lying on its stomach on the sofa, a towel under it and a pillow placed to prevent its rolling off on to the floor. Melody stared down at the tiny form encased in a fuzzy garment.

The man was at the other end of the living-room, moving slowly along the rack of tapes and compact discs, perhaps assessing her, or Robin, by the music that he found there. He had taken his jacket off. Under it he wore a long-sleeved, off-white cotton shirt, the cuffs rolled back to his elbows. His arms matched his shoulders and chest, rock-hard and heavily muscled.

'What did you say your name was?' She moved towards him, wanting to pull him away from that part of the house, into the public part where he would be more easily controlled.

'Alexander,' he said, not looking up. 'Scott Alexander. You've got a lot of Robin Conners's music here, haven't you? I didn't know he'd done some of these albums.' He looked up then, smiling, thinking music instead of babies, it seemed. 'You're a Conners fan. So was Donna.'

His eyes rested on her change of appearance, the smoothly waving hair, the sweater that drowned out her figure. His expression became thoughtful, assessing, and she wondered what she had told him without knowing. She felt an uncomfortable excitement that left her slightly breathless.

She moved to take the compact disc case out of his hand. Incredible, but it seemed that he did not know. She frowned, but it was not her place to tell him. Not yet, anyway. 'The long-playing records are a few years old. I don't think they're available any more. Done before Ro—Conners became popular. I've got all his——' She broke off and asked, 'Would you like a cup of coffee? Then, if you've got some kind of evidence that child is my brother's, perhaps it would be time to bring it out.'

He nodded abruptly and went to the sofa where he had left his jacket beside the baby. She followed him and took the bundle of letters that he held out. She wanted to take it away, to the kitchen or upstairs, somewhere private so that he would not be watching while she read.

She recognised Robin's handwriting. The first letter was dated June of last year, written from the house here.

Last June. Robin had turned up suddenly, storming into the house, taciturn and moody. It had been almost a year since he had spent any time in Queen Charlotte. According to Jeff, all winter Robin had been disappearing after every performance, although no one knew where. Melody had been too tied up in her own priorities to wonder much about either the disappearances or the moody visit in June. Robin's business, she had told herself. If he wanted her to know, he would tell her.

The answer was here, in a letter written by her twin to his love.

You have asked the one thing I can't give you, my darling. I hated the harsh words and anger of our parting, but now, with the anger gone, nothing is changed. Even for you, my love, I can't give up my career. I would not be the man you say you love if I killed that part of myself. I believe that we could make a loving home, a close family, without that sacrifice. If you decide to try, you know always how to reach me. If not,

there's no point in our seeing each other again,
is there? With love, and hope. Robin.

The other letters were older. Written in Robin's hand.
Love-letters. She did not read them.

'How old is the baby?' she asked, whispering.

'Two months.'

Conceived before they parted in anger. Already alive
in Donna's womb when Robin wrote that letter, although
Robin must not have known. Last June. She closed her
eyes and remembered Robin's visit. Two weeks of Robin
at his worst, difficult and moody, prowling the living-
room each morning. Watching for the postman?

She put the letters down, deliberately not handing them
back to him. 'By right those are Robin's.'

He nodded.

She said intensely, 'He didn't know. She must not have
told him about the baby. Robin wouldn't have taken off
if she had.'

'No,' he agreed. 'She didn't tell him. She didn't tell
me, either, who the father was. She said she loved him,
but she couldn't stand to be always like her foster—her
mother had been, always waiting for her husband to
come home.' Then, finally, he answered the question she
had not asked. 'She was my sister. She died ten days
ago.'

'Oh, God,' she whispered. 'Poor Robin.' The baby
shifted, grumbling, and Melody touched the little
shoulder, wondering how she was going to tell Robin.

'Now that you know why, will you tell me how to get
in touch with him?' His hands pushed deeply into his
pockets, his shoulders threatening to burst the seams of
his shirt.

She swallowed. 'You can't. Not now. He's in the
middle of the Pacific.'

'He's a seaman? On a ship?' He became briskly businesslike. 'Radio-telephone? All those big ships have radio communications these days.'

She prowled restlessly to the map of the world that was tacked up over the radio. 'Not a big ship. A little sail-boat. He's halfway to Hawaii on a sail-boat.' She swung back to the man and the baby. 'I can talk to him on amateur radio, but that's as public as shouting in the town square. I can't talk to him about something like this.'

He looked at his watch, frowning, then turned and stared at the sleeping baby. 'I could leave him with you. You're his aunt, after all. You can deliver him to the father.'

She could feel it closing in on her, could feel herself losing control again. How could she ever finish the songs in time if she had a baby to look after? What did she know about babies? She said desperately, 'And you're his uncle. And one hell of a lot more capable of looking after a baby than I am. At least you know how to change nappies, what to do about bottles and formulas. I don't know beans about any of that, and I can't——'

'Oh, for——' He prowled across the carpet, his voice angry but muted to avoid waking the baby. 'What I know about it you could write on a postage stamp. A half-hour with a public health nurse. What she told me, I'll tell you.'

'I——' Poor baby. Robin's baby. Of course, she would have to take care of it. Heaven knew how she would manage to finish the last five songs. She shrugged and said, 'I suppose you have to be back at work some-where. What is your name again?'

'Alexander.' He looked down at the baby and something happened to the harshness in his face. He said, 'I'm due on board ship in three weeks. I had been

planning a trip to Mexico with a friend in the meantime,
but . . .'

She knew she was crazy to suggest it, but in six or seven
days Robin would be in Hawaii, in reach of telephones
and jet transport. Meanwhile, Melody simply had to
work. She expected Mr Alexander to reject the whole
idea, but surprisingly he agreed immediately, as if it were
the most ordinary thing in the world, that two strangers
should share care of one small baby.

She said bluntly, 'You've got to do your share. I'll
help with getting him up, and evenings, and waking up
in the night.' Her voice was brisk, and she wondered
where her firmness was coming from. 'But from eight
in the morning until one in the afternoon, I'm upstairs
working, and little Robin is your problem. Then from
two until four I'm gone.'

'Fair enough,' he agreed. 'As long as you tell your
brother, get him to fly here as soon as he hits Hawaii?'

'Yes.' Robin's baby. Of course she would tell him.

'All right.' He looked around, taking in the rather
formal furnishing. 'I'll get my things from the hotel,
move in here. Do you think you could find a crib or
something for the baby? One of your friends, or——'

'I don't know. I'll try. Mrs Winston might know of
something.' His heavy brows lifted and she explained,
'She comes in once a week to clean. I'll call her and ask.'

He glanced at his watch and grinned. 'Later,' he suggested. 'It's eleven. According to our agreement, you
should be upstairs working.'

She did not like leaving him alone downstairs. She
could see his eyes watching, missing nothing, assessing.
He would prowl through her books and her music, and
somehow that seemed a violation of her private self. She
knew she would not feel that way if Scott were one of

the guests Charlie kept sending up to her. So she went upstairs, telling herself what a crazy fool she was, full of fantasies and foolishness. But upstairs she did not close off the dormer window with soundproofing, and knew it was because she wanted to hear what went on.

She heard his truck when he left. He must have taken the baby with him. She heard when he returned, too, and she left the synthesiser to go to the window. He carried the baby in first, then came back for the suitcase and a bag of groceries. He moved with a competent self-confidence. As if it were *his* home.

She opened the door to the sound-room, opening herself to his sounds. She could hear him walking downstairs. The kitchen. The refrigerator, she thought. The baby cried, but only briefly. He went to it. She heard him moving, and she went back to the synthesiser and stared at the paper, but his presence and the baby's were so strong that she could not get her mind on the words or the music.

One o'clock. She stayed in the music-room until the digital clock read exactly time. Then she went downstairs and he was in the kitchen, cooking.

'Soup,' he said, turning to the sound of her bare feet coming. 'Mushroom soup, and cheese sandwiches. And could you give Robin his bottle?'

'Robin?' She held him, thinking of an endless confusion of names. Donna must have wanted to remember the man she loved, but Melody decided she would call him Robbie. 'Robbie,' she said, aloud, as if christening him.

'Less confusing,' agreed Robbie's uncle as he handed her a warm bottle of milk. She put the nipple in the baby's mouth and the man said, 'No. Hold it like this or he'll get air bubbles.' His hand closed over hers to show her. She felt a jolt, as if he were high voltage.

She felt as if the man were watching her, although whenever she looked up she could see that the soup and the sandwiches were taking far more of his attention than the woman feeding his nephew.

It felt strange, this small life in her arms. How had she got to the age of thirty without ever holding a baby in her arms?

After lunch he settled Robbie on the sofa, then went to move his truck so that she could get her van out. He backed the truck out and stopped in the turn-around, smiling at her, lifting his hand as she reversed past him. As if it were a routine they went through often, his truck moving for her car.

As if they lived together always.

She drove to the radio station, too fast and too carelessly. If she did not get her mind on the important things, on her driving and her song-writing, she would have an accident. Or Robin would have no songs to sing when the recording sessions began.

Scott Alexander. Scott.

'It's ridiculous to call me Mister,' he had said, laughing when she did, the weathered lines around his eyes crinkling so that she had to smile back at him. 'Or for me to call you Ms. We're related, almost. I'm Scott, and you're Melody.'

He was at ease in her house, did not seem to mind turning his hand to any kind of work from chopping wood to changing nappies. He had started the washing-up as she finished eating. There was really nothing he did that she could object to. He was a helpful guest, and how many of those did she have? They were more likely to be careless and messy. Yet she wished he were not quite so comfortable in her home, as if it were *his* place. She could feel him taking over, could feel herself losing her peace and her solitude.

At the radio station John Wainright had everything ready for the two o'clock *Island Time* programme. John was easy to work with, relaxed and good-humoured. Melody always enjoyed listening to his pleasant baritone, as did the listeners. For her, co-hosting the daily session of *Island Time* was a part-time job, fun and good for keeping herself from getting house-bound. For John, radio was his career and he was a professional in his own laid-back fashion. He did the research, most of the interviews. Melody chose the music. On the air they were a smooth partnership, captivating their audience.

Today John introduced the show, then Melody read the news, followed by the marine weather forecast for the fishermen. She saw Laurie, the station manager, through the glass windows to Studio Two just as she finished the weather. She lifted her hand and Laurie smiled back at her. Everything was going smoothly.

John did a live interview with a Haida Indian chief about land claims, then Melody introduced an Anne Murray song. John threw the switch that brought the song on air and killed their microphones.

'Chief Hall always gives a good interview,' he said, smiling.

Melody glanced at her list of music. 'John, does your baby still use a crib?'

'No.' John chuckled. 'The little beggar kept climbing out and falling, so we put him in a cot. You'll have to come see him. He's not a baby any more, you know. They call them toddlers at this stage.'

'Could I borrow the crib?' She glanced up and saw his eyes dropping to her waist. She snapped, 'No! Don't be silly! A—a house guest.'

'Oh? Different from your usual theatre crowd?'

She shuffled papers, then spread them out in front of her. 'John, please don't ask a bunch of questions.'

He reached for the switch and his voice dropped as he spoke into the microphone. 'That was Anne Murray's latest. In a few minutes we'll be talking to the lighthouse keeper at Langara Island lightstation, where a dramatic rescue took place only yesterday. But first, Melody has more music for us.'

Melody introduced Robin's latest hit song. Few of the islanders knew that Robin Conners and their Robin Connacher were the same person, or that Melody wrote most of his songs. She introduced the song in the same way she would any other, and John brought it on air.

'We gave it away,' he told her as Robin's deep voice went out over the airwaves. 'Well, actually we loaned it, because Bev and I are planning to have another. But we could loan you a playpen. Bev used to use it for a crib when we went travelling.'

So Melody drove home with a collapsed playpen in the back of her van, and Bev's promise to come over the next day to look at the baby and give Melody a few tips on baby-care. Bev had not asked any questions. John must have told her that Melody did not want to talk. Not that it was a secret, exactly, but it seemed Robin's place to acknowledge the little baby as his child, not Melody's.

That night the radio interference was even worse than the night before. Melody could not hear anything but static. 'We'll have to try tomorrow,' she told Scott as she switched the transceiver off.

Scott was sitting in the chair across from her, his legs crossed, the fabric of his jeans pulled tightly over his muscular thighs. He had a history of the Queen Charlotte Islands in his hands. Laurie, the station manager, had given Melody the book last Christmas. Melody tried to think of her home back to normal, of the chair across from her empty and the man gone.

Soon. A few days and she would be able to move from room to room without seeing Scott Alexander. She shook her head slightly, trying to clear the images. As if he would always be there, the ghost of a man she hardly knew, haunting her with all the things that she was not born to be. She looked away from him, focusing on the transceiver she had switched off. The silence was full of whispers and murmurs and he could hear and understand all of them.

Nervously, she said, 'Ham radio's like that. The bands are good one day, bad the next. Sometimes it takes a few days, but I'll get through to Robin some time this week.'

Earlier, while she was at the station, Scott had chopped wood. The fireplace was crackling now, sending out a flow of warm air and the aroma of burning spruce. He had laid the fire while she was gone, and she had felt the warmth the instant she came through the door.

She wished he were not so helpful. In an odd way it threw her off balance. He set the book aside and moved along the shelves of records and tapes and compact discs. Her music, and Robin's, and their parents'. He took out a disc and she wanted to scream at him to get out, stop touching and looking and setting her nerves on edge.

The tension had been building inside her all evening. She could feel every movement he made as an abrasive scratch on the surface of her mind. He opened a plastic case and took a disc out, his callused fingers careful on the shining plastic. He put it into the player. Then the music filled the room and she forgot that she was irritated at the way he was taking over her home. It was Robin's voice, singing his first hit song, 'Girl on the Road'. The song touched Melody, as it always had, and she fell back in her seat, silent, listening.

He must have touched buttons on the stereo when the piece was over, because there was silence, the crackle of the fire and a small explosion of coloured flame, but not the opening notes of the second piece on the album.

'You should have told me,' he said quietly. His voice struck her with the sting of a subdued slap.

'Told you what?'

She twisted her hands together in her lap. He was a stranger, but he was slipping through the secrets and the barriers. She tensed as he walked over to her, but he only dropped a small leaflet into her lap, the insert from the album.

'That your brother is really Robin Conners.'

She had almost told him.

He bent over her, his fingers brushing hers as he opened the little leaflet. His voice was not soft now, but harsh and angry. 'There are the words to the songs, and the credits, or whatever you call them. "Girl on the Road" was written by Melody Connacher. That's your name. Your brother's name is Robin. It's a bit too much of a coincidence otherwise, isn't it? Conners. Connacher. A stage name.'

She stared at the paper, at his hand still holding it. There was a faint white scar on the side of his thumb. She said unsteadily, 'There was no reason to tell you. It wasn't your business.' She drew in a big breath, and added, 'You didn't ask.'

He had told her his sister was a fan of Robin Conners. That was the time for her to say, No wonder, because Robin and Robin are one and the same. The words were there between them, talk without sound, his accusation and her lack of defence.

Why should it matter? Somehow, it did. His eyes had turned to granite and her throat was dry and aching with something crazily like tears. She could feel the anger in him, could sense the instant when it burst, silently. She winced, from nothing more than feelings on the air, and he turned abruptly and walked out of the living-room.

She did not follow him, although her hands reached out as if to stop him. She heard the creak of the fourth step as he went upstairs. All right. Better that way, because now there was no need to feel she had to entertain him, to hover around when she would rather be alone.

Why did she feel as if she had done something hurtful? He was the one who was out of line, getting angry about nothing.

She turned off the lights and locked the doors, checked the windows. Not many people in Queen Charlotte worried about locking doors, but Melody was always aware of living alone, and with the doors and windows locked she felt more comfortable.

She went upstairs. The door to the bedroom she had given him was closed. She went into Robin's room where she had put the playpen. The baby was a soft, small, motionless form, lying on his stomach and breathing through his mouth. She stood staring down at little Robbie for a long time.

Tomorrow she would tell Scott Alexander that he could go. She would get Mrs Wilson in to help. There was no reason why she couldn't look after Robin's baby alone. She would far rather have that man out of her house, her world back to normal.

She bent down and touched the fine black hair on the baby's head. She thought of Amanda saying that it was silly to give children their parents' names, that it only led to confusion. Little Robin. Robbie. She wondered if Amanda would be a sucker for a baby, and discovered she had no idea how her mother felt about babies.

She wondered where it was that Scott Alexander had to be in three weeks' time. On board a ship, he had said.

It didn't sound much like a fishing boat, which had been her first guess. She wondered who the friend was, the one he had planned to go to Mexico with.

She went into her music-room and closed the door. She closed the shutters, too, and finally, in the quiet of the night, she was able to work.

She woke early, before the alarm rang. She lay still for a moment, listening to the whisper of wind in the trees outside. The house was silent except for the faint creaking that an old wooden building gave in the night. Even the wind outside was faint, rustlings through the spruce needles interspersed with magic silences.

She heard the baby then, a faint grumble that was closer than the wind. If he had woken earlier, she had not heard him. She slipped out of bed, her bare feet on the cool floor, and went to Robin's room.

The door to Scott's room was open slightly, as if to allow him to hear if Robbie cried. Melody slipped past the open door silently and went into the baby's room. She lifted the small, grumbling form up and cuddled him to her while she got a nappy out of the package. She changed him while he waved his chubby legs and arms aimlessly and made gurgling noises at her. She felt ridiculously pleased that she managed the small task without mishap.

She carried Robbie down to the kitchen, feeling more relaxed down there. She was less likely to wake Scott. There was an empty, dirty baby bottle in the sink, evidence that Scott had been up in the night with the baby.

She thought of his open door. She had left her own door open, too. Had Scott looked in on her in the middle of the night, staring at her sleeping form tangled in the covers? Was that why she had slept so restlessly? Why was she so aware of him? It was never like this with the strangers Charlie sent to visit. Even Jeff's visits hardly disturbed her work. She left him to his own devices when she wanted to work, sought him out when she felt like having a friend around.

She mixed the formula and heated a new bottle. Then she settled into her favourite chair by the stereo while Robbie curled against her and sucked noisily at his breakfast.

He fell asleep right afterwards, so she put him on the sofa as Scott had, with a pillow to stop him rolling off. She got herself breakfast then, a spoonful of honey over fresh yoghurt. Then she went back upstairs and dressed hurriedly, suddenly nervously certain that Scott would wake any moment, and aware of how little the T-shirt did to cover her.

Scott was still sleeping at eight; at least he had not come out of his room. Their deal said that it was his turn to look after the baby now while Melody worked. She grimaced at his door, but actually she preferred it this way, with him sleeping, out of her way.

She moved the playpen into the sound-room, careful not to bang it or make any noise. Then she brought Robbie up and closed the door, locking it because if the baby would be quiet she wanted to record this morning. She didn't want anyone walking in and throwing opening-door sounds over the six-string guitar.

Of course, he might knock loudly on the locked door, and that would ruin the recording, too. If he did interrupt, she would go up in flames and that would be the last time he would interfere with Melody Connacher when she was working!

She grinned at a vision of herself screaming at that muscular hulk of a he-man. Best done in fantasy, she decided.

'Time you got used to music,' she told the baby as she lowered him on his back into the play pen. He grinned and gurgled as she played back last night's work, and she warned him, 'Talk all you want now, but once the listening's done and I start laying the percussion track on, you behave and keep quiet.'

He squirmed and his mouth twisted, and Melody decided that it *was* a smile on his lips.

She had recorded the bass guitar last night, then layered the drums on top of the bass, using her multi-track recorder. Now she listened, and it was good. The rhythm was filling, the music gaining depth. She changed the disk in the synthesiser and played with the controls until she had the percussion sounds she wanted. She made notes on her paper while Robin groaned and grunted and whimpered.

She picked him up and raised him to her shoulder as she had seen Scott do the night before, remembering just in time to put a towel over her shoulder. Robin groaned, then burped sour milk on to her towel. She patted his back and congratulated him. Then his wide, dark eyes dropped and she put him down on his stomach. He twitched once, then promptly fell asleep.

The percussion layer went on like smooth butter on a sandwich. She worked, unaware of time passing, until it was finished. Then she played the recording back and knew that the words were not quite right. The second stanza would have to be changed to follow the rhythm and the mood. She played it again, humming the words. Then again, and suddenly the right phrase came to her.

It was almost eleven when Robin squirmed and grunted. Melody picked him up and rocked him with one arm while she finished her notes. Working with a baby in the house was going to be a breeze. She should have known, because Amanda and Charlie had sung their way around the world, dragging twin babies with them, and it had not visibly cramped their style. And as for the babies, she and Robin were healthy enough, normal enough. If Amanda could do it, Melody surely could.

Robin started to cry. Melody murmured, 'OK, I know. You want a new nappy.'

Scott was there in the hall when she came out of the sound-room with the baby. 'I'll take him,' he said coolly, and his eyes were granite again this morning.

'It's OK.' She shook her head and dodged his hands. 'I'll look after him.'

She walked past Scott, into Robin's room, the room that belonged now to both the small Robbie and her twin. She changed the nappy and Scott stood in the doorway, watching but not smiling at her this morning, just staring.

Finally he spoke, his voice cool and formal. 'I slept in.'

Robbie waved his legs and got the nappy snarled up before she could fasten the tapes. Without looking at Scott, she said neutrally, 'You said you were short of sleep yesterday.' She felt a tight band across her chest and wished he were smiling at her again. She felt as if she had lost something precious, and that was crazy.

'It's time for you to be working. I'll look after Robin now.'

'No need.' She managed the nappy the second time, and snapped up the legs of his all-in-one. She picked the baby up and held him in her arms like a shield as she faced Scott. 'He's not difficult.'

'He can be,' said Scott wryly.

The man was too big. He filled the doorway and made no move to let her past. She stopped, holding the baby tightly as she looked at him, wondering if she had imagined the warmth in those eyes yesterday.

She said, 'I've been thinking about it. You're right. There's no reason you can't leave Robbie with me. I can look after him.' She looked down at the tiny head. 'Consider him handed over. There's no need for you to stay.'

He didn't like it. She didn't know why. Yesterday he had wanted to push Robbie into her arms and walk away. Now he said, 'You go out every afternoon. You can't park Robbie in a playpen at the radio station.'

Amanda and Charlie had parked their babies in all sorts of places, many of them more chaotic than a modern radio station. She hugged Robbie closer and said, 'There's Mrs Winston. She can come in and look after Robbie while I'm out.'

'And the mornings? When you're in your music studio upstairs?'

She had not told him what was up there, in that room. Damn it, she had not told him much at all, but he seemed to know.

She snapped, 'Robbie's fine with me. Would you let me past? Please! I want to take him downstairs.'

At first she thought he would stop her, but he stepped back and she stumbled past, catching herself before she tripped. She got to the stairs before she realised that the playpen was in the music-room, that she had been working and had only stopped to change the baby. She turned and went back, and thankfully Scott was gone. The door to his room was closed.

She shut herself into the sound-room with the baby. Was he packing? She hoped so. He would go, and she would be alone with Robbie, and her life could return to normal. A new normal with her brother's child to care for. She supposed she should go back and ask Scott for his address, because she should send him word of his nephew from time to time. He would probably want to know how the child grew, although he had been quick enough to try to hand the baby over yesterday.

She had the sense not to try to lay the next track on to the new song. Not with her fingers trembling as if she and Scott had been screaming at each other out there. He had not even raised his voice, so why did she feel so shattered?

She played the recording back, then played it again. She made notes, but she would not touch the synthesiser until he was gone. 'You understand, don't you, Robbie?' she asked the baby as she took the soundproofing off the window. 'I'm not a stage type, like your dad or your grandparents. They can turn it on under pressure, but I need peace and quiet.'

Robbie gurgled and squirmed in agreement.

She picked him up and carried him downstairs in the end, because she really should be down there when Scott left, to get his address and say thanks and goodbye.

The door to Scott's room was still closed, or closed again. He was probably finished with it, had cleared it out, although she knew he had not started the truck outside. He must be downstairs. She could feel him in her house, knew he was not gone. He was like that, impossible to ignore, intruding without actually doing anything she could put her finger on.

He was in the living-room, prowling along the bookshelves. He had out a book and was standing, turning the pages. That was what bothered her, because he had not asked if he could read the books, had not asked before he played her music. She knew that Charlie's stray friends never asked, but somehow it was different with Scott. She put the baby down on the sofa again.

She said, 'I thought you would be gone by now.' She was shocked at the rudeness in her own voice.

His whole face was rigid, and his voice. 'I'm sticking around. I want to meet your brother before I entrust my nephew to his care.'

She gasped, then snapped, 'You weren't so fussy yesterday. You were in a hurry to hand over your problem and get the hell out of here.'

He swung away from her, going to the window. He sounded like the sea captain she had fancied he was, handing out decisions, orders. 'But I've had second thoughts. So, Ms Connacher, I'm afraid that I'm staying, whether you like it or not.' He turned and faced her. Arrogant, she thought. Bossy. She did not like him.

She glared at him and he stared back, and there was no way he was leaving. Short of her calling the police and having him thrown out, Scott Alexander was staying.

She said, 'I don't like it. I don't want you here.'

'I know.' Lines drawn between them. Battle lines, although what was there to fight about? He said, 'Don't worry, I'll survive it. It won't be the first time I've stuck around when I wasn't wanted.'

There was something ominous about the way he said the words, as if the man's will was as strong as his body. Easy to get along with yesterday when he seemed to approve of her. But since last night there had been coolness and anger instead of a friendship in its infancy. She was trying to send him away, and he was damned if he would go.

'Better,' he said softly, 'if you don't fight me. I'm staying.'

She could call John, ask him to come and throw out her unwanted guest. But John was too civilised for that kind of aggressive act, and he was her workmate, not a man to run to. There was Luke, Laurie's husband. Luke and Scott would probably be about a match for each other, both tough and hard and mostly hidden inside themselves.

Would they actually fight? Would Scott go that far, physically insisting on staying, even to the point of a fist fight?

Luke would want to know why, so would anyone she asked to help. She would sound like an idiot, because Scott would smile as he had yesterday and anyone would wonder just what her problem was. The baby's uncle, and she herself had invited him to stay only yesterday. She would never be able to voice the way this man made her feel, as if he could crush her will with one of those muscular hands.

'So I'll stay,' he said, conversationally but coolly. He turned the book in his hands. 'I'll enjoy your library. You've several books I've wanted to read.'

She wanted to hit him, but her small fists would make no more impression than her screaming voice.

'We have a deal, of course,' he said tonelessly. 'It's time for you to be upstairs writing Robin Connors' next hit song, isn't it? I'm the baby-minder, and I'll make lunch. How about a quiche?'

Her lips twitched and she felt the tension flowing away like a mysterious, wild river. He was smiling, saying, 'I know. "Real men don't eat quiche". I've heard that one. We'll call it egg pie, shall we?'

She realised then that he had won. He had turned her anger into laughter, and he was staying. She turned her smile to a frown and walked out of the room. There was nothing she could say that would not acknowledge his victory, so she would be silent.

CHAPTER FOUR

MELODY tried to pretend he was not there. Hopeless, but she managed a cool distance. Polite coexistence with Scott, while he chopped wood and devoured her music and her books, smiled coolly and made her uncomfortably aware that she was behaving badly.

He asked if he could use her telephone to make some long-distance calls, adding, 'I'll put them on my calling card, of course.'

'Why bother asking?' she snapped, wishing the words unsaid. He had been polite. She was the irrational one, telling him to stay, then turning surly and irritated at his presence in her home.

He called someone named Caroline. His wife, for all she knew. She heard him say the name and she walked away, not listening, or trying not to, but she felt relieved that his voice on the telephone sounded cool, not loving. He made other calls, but she made sure that she did not hear them.

Bev came on Wednesday morning and looked at the baby. Bev was a nurse and a mother herself, the nearest thing to an expert that Melody had available. Bev and Robbie gurgled at each other, then Bev asked Scott questions about formulas and nap times.

Scott and Bev seemed to like each other on sight. Melody felt uncomfortably tense listening to the easy conversation between her friend and Scott. He had hardly smiled in two days, and now he was laughing when Bev asked him how the baby had travelled, telling her about his disastrous trip north on the ferry.

He hadn't told Melody about the trip at all.

She felt like a child, left out, not knowing how to get in, telling herself she did not care. Bev was being friendly, and he was being the charming man he obviously could be without much trouble. No wonder he preferred to talk to Bev. Melody had frowned and snapped and, perhaps, even sulked. No wonder he had none of those smiles for her, with the laughter sparking in the crinkles around his eyes, breaking out in his low voice.

'What are you?' Bev asked, laughing at his account of trying to nurse a baby on a heaving ferry. 'You're a seaman, aren't you?'

He nodded. 'Master of an icebreaker in the Beaufort Sea.'

Melody supposed that he would have told her if she had asked.

Scott Alexander. Hard body and smiling eyes that could turn to stone. Dangerous. Bev obviously did not think so, but Melody had felt unsettled ever since she opened her door to him. Even when she was away at the radio station, just thinking about coming back, she could feel turmoil inside her.

Her instincts for self-preservation told her to deal with him as she had the other unsettling influences in her life. Shut him out. She tried.

On Wednesday night the net frequency was nothing but a mass of static. Melody had a noise level of twenty over nine, hopeless for talking to anyone. She wondered how long it would be before she could talk to Robin again.

Scott gave the baby his feed as Melody was trying the radio, then put him to bed. Melody disappeared into her music-room while Scott was in the bedroom with Robbie. She worked alone until eleven, then went silently to bed. Her new policy, she decided. She was avoiding Scott

Alexander. Much easier on her equilibrium if she did not see him. The light was shining up the stairs from the living-room, so she tiptoed silently past the stairwell to her own room and closed the door.

She lay for a long time in the dark, listening to the sounds of trees and wind and a fine rain outside. Scott was very quiet downstairs. She closed her eyes and tried to form shapes and colours, to drift on a dreamy tide of music to a place far away.

She jerked back to consciousness abruptly, lay awake listening to nothing, then the soft sound of a man's tread outside her door. A board creaked. A light switched on. She saw the crack of brightness under her bedroom door. She was very still, breathing very quietly, trying to catch at sleep again, not listening yet hearing every step he took.

He walked across the hallway to the baby's room. Silence, hushed. Back to the room he slept in. She had to stop thinking of it as *Scott's* room. It was not anybody's room. A spare bedroom. An assortment of people had used it. Robin's friends. Her parents' friends who turned up saying, 'Hello, Charlie said you might have a bed for me for a few nights. Just passing through, getting away from it all. Resting, you know.'

She had put up so many of them since she came back here. After all, Amanda and Charlie had sent a string of guests up here over the years. Most of them had been tended to by Mrs Winston who had lived in until Melody came back to take up residence.

Melody lay in her bed in the darkness, not listening, or trying not to listen, for Scott's sounds, trying to make sense of her own strange reaction to this one man. All those friends of her parents, friends of Robin's. She had invited them in and said, 'Here's the bed, and there's the kitchen. Help yourself. The beach is that way, four blocks downhill. Make yourself at home, just remember that if the door to the sound-room is closed, *don't knock on it and don't open it!*'

None of them had disturbed her peace, not since she had learned to stop feeling guilty about putting her work first. So what was different about this one man with his easy smile and his impenetrable eyes?

The crack of light under her door disappeared. The house groaned. She could hear a slow drip, water in the drainpipe. A very light rain, typical of the misty isles.

She must have slept. The sound of rain was gone when she opened her eyes again. There was soft light through her window from the rising moon. Her bedroom window looked out on the forest and she never closed her blinds.

There was no sound at all, not even the house making night groans. She got up and went silently barefoot to the baby. She had forgotten to open her door. He might have cried and she would not have heard. Scott would have heard, she supposed, because his door was open a crack.

Robbie was just starting to stir when she got there. She lifted him and changed him while he was still half asleep and had not found his voice yet. Then she carried him dowstairs, because it was time for his night feed. Scott usually woke for this one. Melody seldom heard the baby until later in the morning.

She warmed the bottle, then went back upstairs, settling on her brother's bed with pillows behind her, holding the baby in her arms. Watching the little mouth sucking intently, she relaxed into a half-sleep herself. She had never really thought about having babies. It had not seemed to go with her life.

She tilted the bottle to stop little Robin from sucking air, drew her leg up to support the baby's little bottom.

He was so small, curled into the curve of her arm, his legs lying across her abdomen.

There was no sound, but she felt her heart stop, then smash into her ribs. She looked up and he was there. Scott. Standing in the doorway, looking at her. There was no light, but the moonlight was bathing her in a pale gleam.

She licked her lips without realising, staring at him. He was in shadow, a black form in the doorway. He moved and she could see the lines of him, the smoothness of his broad shoulders telling her that he wore no shirt. Then he came closer, and she could see him in sharp silhouette. He had put on his jeans, but she would swear he wore nothing else. He stood stiffly, watching her as if she held his attention against his will. Staring at her.

Her eyes flew down, to the baby in her arm, to the pale nakedness of her legs curled casually across the bed, the white edge of her T-shirt against her upper thigh. He moved and she jerked her gaze up, and now the moonlight showed his face, still and intent on her. She did not need to look down now, to know what he saw. Her free breasts, swelling under the thin cotton knit of the shirt. The baby pushed his fist into her breast and she heard Scott take in a shaken breath.

'Melody...'

It was just a whisper. She had never heard his voice like that, lower than ever, filled with tenderness and desire.

Somehow, she must move, must talk and break this spell. She swallowed and licked her dry lips, and his eyes were on her throat, her lips. She could see him clearly now, and his man's body did not try to hide that he wanted her. He had hardly touched her, not even casually, in the days he had been her guest, but right now his eyes were blazing through the moonlit room.

It was the moonlight. Her fault, not thinking to put on a robe. She shifted the baby and tried to arrange herself more modestly, but it was impossible because she was wearing next to nothing. The moonlight showed every curve she had in its sensuous, gentle glow.

'I——' Her voice sounded like his, low and seductive, like an invitation. She cleared her throat and said, 'It's all right. I'm feeding him.' He didn't move and she stumbled on, 'S—Scott . . . you can go back to bed. You don't need——'

Bed. She half choked, her arms on the baby. The bottle made a noise and she shifted it, but it was empty. How could she get up without that shirt shifting even higher on her hips?

Scott said, 'He's done that bottle. Give him to me and I'll put him back to bed.' His voice was normal now, but his eyes weren't normal. They were heated and filled with golden fire. She gulped as he reached down for the baby.

She scrambled to her feet. Scott turned to lay the baby in the playpen. Better, she thought in relief. The shirt hung halfway down her thighs now. She was uncomfortably aware that her breasts were two soft, sensuous swellings free under the soft knit, but when she started to cross her arms over them he stood up and she saw his smile growing, but it was more than a smile. It was a touch, a caress.

He said softly, 'That just makes it more obvious.'

She gasped softly and looked down, saw that she had pushed the swelling of her breasts up and dropped her arms abruptly. 'I—you—I'd better go back to . . . Goodnight!'

She moved, quickly. He moved, too. She stopped abruptly, but he was only half an arm's length away, between her and the door. She could see the bulge of his chest muscles, his heavy biceps pressing against his naked chest. She looked down, could not seem to stop herself, and his chest hair thickened as she followed it, then thinned as it trailed down to the waist of his jeans.

He had not taken time to put his belt on.

He was watching her, seeing everything. The way his naked chest affected her, her own awareness of his eyes on her. Her body, breasts swelling in some mysterious woman's reaction to this man's chemistry. There were no words, but so much said. He was closer, and in a second his lips would take hers. She felt it coming. Not his hands on her. She thought she would jump, run away, if his hands touched, but he held that back.

The softest brush of hard, full lips against hers. She shivered and the touch returned, brushing, caressing, light, not demanding. She tried to breathe and she could not. She tried to step back, but he had her trapped with only those teasing lips.

'Scott——' It was a gasp, air sucked in, his name distorted. His tongue slipped in, taking advantage of her whisper, a warm invasion along her inner lips. She tried to say his name, a protest, but the sound might have been anything. Her heart was panicked, thundering. Her chest felt like the frightened trembling of a sparrow.

He stepped back before the shivering could grow to push him away. Her eyes flew wide, staring at him, and he said softly, 'Stop looking at me like a trapped animal. You're free.'

She did not feel it. She was at the mercy of his touch, her breath falling into short, quick gulps as she saw his hands move and thought of his touch sliding along her screaming nerves.

He caught her wrists lightly and turned them, his thumbs stroking her inner wrist where the pulse throbbed, his eyes holding hers. She could not even seem to find the will to look away, although she could feel her pupils widening as his light touch caressed the soft flesh that led towards her inner elbow.

'Melody,' he said on a whisper. 'With a name like that, I should have known you'd be all softness and nerves.' He swallowed and she could feel his lips on hers, but he did not move. Just his fingers, sliding along her arms, sending her body trembling with heat.

She had to get away, wanted to get away, but it was she who moved closer as his callused fingers slid along her bare upper arms, fingertips sliding under the sleeves of her shirt, wrists brushing the fullness of her nearby breasts.

Then his lips were close and her breath turned to a gasp as he bent down to take her mouth. She shuddered, felt him tremble, and his hands closed on her arms, pulling her against his hard chest, trapping her hands which had somehow found their way into the curling hairs on his chest.

She tried to stare up at him, to say something that needed to be said, some protest perhaps, but his mouth took hers in a deep invasion that she could only return as her body sought the hard contours of his.

Moonlight. Starlight. The heavens spinning, something wild surging up inside her. His tongue explored the gift of her mouth and she learned that there were wild, shattering sensations that could curl along her nerves just from the touch of tongue and teeth, lips that made hers engorge and tremble with sensations of flame and a deep, shuddering urge to surrender more, to feel more, to drown in sensation.

His hands, sliding along her back, claiming her flesh, branding her with his hardness, the rough gentleness of his chest hair through the thin cotton, the gasping surrender that exploded in her when his hands slid to her hips and pulled her closely against his implacable need.

His groan, against her face, in her ear. 'Oh, God, Melody, how can you do this to a man?'

Her head fell back, somehow against his shoulder, her eyes opening slowly, unwillingly. His voice was hardly a whisper.

'Your lips always look like . . . as if they're waiting for a man's kiss. Full and red and sensuous.' He took them and she lost the reality her mind had started to grasp for.

Sensation. Warmth. The wonderful, deep trembling of heated need. Her hands found some freedom as he shifted to caress the curve of her back, the calluses on his fingers scratching slightly on the cotton of her T-shirt as they explored lightly the shape of her spine, the hint of her ribs, the full swellings that were her free breasts.

She gasped and suddenly she was heavy in his hands, his fingers forming her breasts, holding them up for the soft seeking of his lips. She groaned in the instant his lips touched. The cloth was not a barrier, but a teasing, sensuous tool, passing the warmth of his breath, the seeking firmness of his lips. She was trembling, her fingers clenching in the hair of his chest to try to keep some kind of sanity . . . her legs, weak and trembling, collapsing against his as he brought her hips close with one arm, holding her firm and safe from falling, but losing all feeling for up or down or . . .

She heard it, her voice but not hers, a moan that invited touching, kissing, possession. He heard it, felt it, and swept her up into his hard arms. Her head fell back against his arm, his shoulder, and she saw his face above her, a tenseness that was holding some kind of control. He swallowed, and she saw the spasm all along his throat, and the control, what there was of it, was going to end when he got her through that door, into that room.

On to his bed. She felt the softness as he lowered her and she scrambled, breathing shallowly through her mouth, coming off the bed on the other side and halfway to her feet, in a crouch like an animal facing a hunter.

'I...I...' She gulped in air, her hands out as if to ward him off although he was still, watching her, waiting for—for what? 'I—Scott, I—I didn't mean to—to—to do this.'

'This?' He rounded the end of the bed and when she jerked away, she found herself held by one hand, fingers around her wrist like a steel band. He said steadily, 'I didn't see you fighting me off.'

She shook her head, feeling the storm inside herself, the tension that she thought would be with her all through the night. God! She did not even know the man, and his touch, his kiss, had sent her wild. She would have done anything, given anything. Even now she was not sure that it would be different. If his fingers gentled to a caress, the shuddering need could overwhelm her and she would be at his mercy.

She realised from the way he was watching her that her breathing had turned into short gasps, as if he were caressing her. She whispered, 'Please, just—just let go of me and——'

His fingers tightened and she gasped. He released her abruptly and stepped back, but he was the other man, his eyes cold and his voice without the tenderness there had been only moments ago.

'You ask for it, wandering around in that bit of nothing.' His breathing was still heavy, but under control now. 'I see you go past every morning, walking past my door in your bare feet and bare legs, that shirt on as if it were clothing.' He reached his hands and traced the curves of her body, his hands neither gentle nor rough, his voice bringing heat to her cheeks. 'A man's only got to look at you moving to know what's underneath.' His hands found the swelling of her breasts and his fingers stilled, cupping, lifting to make the swelling more prominent. 'One message a man does not get, watching you walk past in that rig, is *no*.'

She gulped, feeling the hard response of her nipples to his touch, staring at the chill of his eyes, knowing they were cold although the moon was draining its light away from the room as it slid behind a cloud.

She whispered, 'I didn't—I just didn't think. I—I grew up in the theatre. Clothes, or the lack of them, didn't mean all that much.' She was talking fast, desperately, stumbling over her own words. 'Changing-rooms and people . . . people running in and out. I——'

His hands freed her. 'Melody, this is no theatre. Don't issue invitations unless you mean them. Not to me.'

She stared at him, nodded but could not get words out. He moved and there was room. She walked past him, out of his room, not looking back, but knowing, feeling, his eyes on her every step of the way.

Somehow, she got to her room and closed her door before she sagged against it and let the trembling of her body take over. So that was it. She had tried to call it distrust, discomfort with his easy way of settling into her home. She had never thought to call it sex. Physical attraction, the kind you read about, the sort of thing she had written songs about without knowing. The sort of emotion that knocked a girl off her moorings and left her trembling and aching for a man's touch.

She had never felt like this before. She shuddered, remembering how she had stepped into his arms. Maybe he was right. She had been teasing him, wandering around, past his open door, never really thinking that he might be awake and watching. Wanting her. Certainly there was no excuse for what she had done tonight. Lying with Robbie on the bed, hardly dressed herself. Had some part of her known he would wake and come? Had she wanted him to come?

He was more honest, reaching to take what she seemed to be advertising. Useless to pretend he had swept her away, carried her into his room against her will. What had he done? The lightest of kisses that shook her to her foundations, then a teasing caress of her bare arms with his fingers. She was the one who had flowed into his arms, who had given up her lips, had groaned his name and wanted, ached for, the touches, the caresses, the kisses.

And the loving.

He had only been about to take what she had seemed to offer. She hugged herself, wondering how she was going to face him in the morning, how she was ever going to get through the days from now until he left. Even now, that crazy part of her wanted to go back to his room, to accept what was in his eyes and his touch and his kiss, and to ask him to love her, to take away the ache that was consuming her.

She heard his step in the hall outside her door and her breathing stopped. Was he coming to her? If he did . . .

She felt herself trembling and knew that if he came to her now, she would not send him away. By morning, she thought, she might have the strength to know what was sanity and what foolishness, but tonight all she could feel was the echo of his touch. Sensation had drowned out thought.

* * *

He almost reached for her doorknob. His fingers were stretched out, curving to take possession of it. Would her door be locked against him?

Then he was past her doorway, going down the stairs, and the moment of insanity was behind him. He was not a randy teenager, unable to control his passions. He certainly did not need to reach out for a woman who swung wildly from giving to a virginal nervousness.

The night had turned clear and fresh after the earlier drizzle. He had intended to take his truck, to drive north along the narrow, winding highway that followed the east coast of Graham Island. But her van was parked behind his truck, and short of shoving the truck into four-wheel drive and putting big tyre tracks all over Melody's front lawn, he was stuck there until he could get her to move her van.

He walked down the hill to the intersection with the next street, then down a long curve to the highway, and finally to the water.

The shore here was barren, rocky and empty. The moon shone to show him his way. He walked until he found a lonely point of high rock, looking out over the water. He stopped then, staring out at the shadow of mountains to the south, across the harbour.

After a while he felt the peace of the night, could feel himself relaxing. He studied the sky, the oldest pastime of seamen. Polaris, of course, lying in the northern sky, higher than she would lie when he looked out from the deck of his ship. Orion there, lying low against the horizon.

What was it about the stars that brought calmness to him? The fact that the stars had not changed in their constellations? He grinned at that thought, but back there, with Melody warm and willing in his arms, the world and the heavens had shifted and he had almost gone spinning out of control.

Part moonlight, perhaps, although she had affected him from that first sight. She was part poet and part sorceress, he thought. Not the kind of woman he was accustomed to reaching for, not what he wanted when passion cleared his senses enough for him to see clearly.

Better by far for him to leave, to entrust little Robbie to her care and go back to a world where he knew the rules. Back to Caroline, who satisifed his needs without threatening the fabric of his life. Back to his half-built home on Cortes Island. Back to his work, piloting ships through the short northern summer.

That had been his intention when he came, to hand the child over as quickly as possible. Except that Robbie had become a person to him now, a small bundle of gurgles and helplessness that he could not abandon. And the father had become an unknown quantity. Robin Connacher, known only in his love-letters to Donna, had seemed a safe guardian for his young nephew. Robin Conners, emerging superstar singer, was another matter.

Scott picked up a stone and threw it into the water, watched the ripples move outwards, flowing along the moonlit, glassy ocean. He was fooling himself. Doubts about Melody's brother were only an excuse. He had commanded men long enough to know them with an unerring instinct. The man who had written those letters to Donna would not fail his own child. And Melody herself would certainly provide any warmth and love that might be lacking from the child's father. Hadn't he watched her holding the baby, her eyes wide and filled with tenderness and warmth as she looked down at Robbie in her arms? No, it was not Robbie's needs that kept him here. The baby would have the kind of stability and love that Donna had never had.

It was time he was honest with himself. From the moment he had stood on the steps of that old wooden house and stared at the tousled woman who opened the door to him with sleep-softened lips and wide, startled eyes, there had been a part of him, unacknowledged, that had known he had to have her. Despite Caroline, although to be honest he and Caroline had never exchanged promises of faithfulness. Despite anyone else who might stand in the way. Despite even Melody herself. Before he could walk away from this place, he must hold Melody Connacher in his arms, kiss those full red lips to swollen surrender, caress that seductive, soft-firm body to wild abandon, and possess her. Totally.

If it could be quick and clean and sudden, he thought, it would be over then. Tonight, if she had not drawn back, they would have been one in an explosion that would have shaken them both to the core, but in the morning it would have been over, and he would be able to walk away.

Now he was uneasy. He knew he was not going to do the sensible thing, was not going to leave, to run while he could. He was going to have her. His mind was already playing with ways to woo her, to seduce her into his bed— into her bed, actually.

He knew that the lovers' game of pursuit and seduction could turn to high explosives when the woman was Melody. He might win her surrender, then spend his nights forever staring up at the stars, remembering her soft heat in his arms, her eyes sliding through his walls.

Whatever peace Scott found staring at the stars over Queen Charlotte harbour, he lost it the next morning when the telephone rang. Melody was upstairs working in the music-room, so he answered.

'Is Melody there?' It was a man who was obviously startled to hear a strange voice.

'Sorry,' he said coolly, feeling an instant and inexplicable antagonism. 'She can't come to the phone right now. Can I give her a message?'

'Damn,' said the voice amiably. 'I thought I might get through early enough. She's working? She usually doesn't get in there until about nine in the morning.'

Scott snapped, 'Yes.' Whoever this was, he was evidently intimate with Melody's habits. 'Yes,' he repeated, his voice under control, and he tried to scorn his own possessive feelings. As if she were his. 'She usually comes out about one. If you—— '

'OK. Ask her to call Jeff at home in LA, would you? I—no, damn it! That won't do. I'll be—look, who is this?'

'Scott Alexander,' he said abruptly.

A pause, then a half-laugh, and Scott felt like a stiff, awkward fool. 'All right, Scott. I'm Jeff.' The friendly voice ignored Scott's stiffness. 'Ask her to call me at Peter's between one and two, could you? If she doesn't, I'll try to catch her this evening.'

Scott delivered the message to Melody at lunch, his voice stiff. She had not met his eyes at breakfast, and did not now. He wondered why the hell he was staying around. Last night's explosive touching seemed like a far country now. There was only tension and, in Melody, no warmth at all.

No warmth, that was, until he said, 'Jeff called.'

'When?' Her lips parted and her eyes lit. He felt even more angry at the confident voice on the telephone. She asked quickly, 'Where is he? Is he coming up here?'

Scott shrugged angrily. 'He wants you to call him between one and two, at Peter's.' He walked away then, but he could hear her voice carrying through the house.

Everything was in her voice, her thoughts and her feelings. When she spoke, he always felt as if he had known her forever.

She was cool now, businesslike. 'Yes, it's Melody—no, I haven't, not yet. I keep telling you, registering it just slows it down. Registered goes through Toronto, and then Vancouver—I called for Jeff. Is he there?'

Then her words quickened, the warmth flowing through the telephone to the man who had called. He must have said something almost at once to make her laugh.

'Yes,' she said lightly, teasing. 'You told me to, and I'm doing my best. What's up?'

Scott shoved the plug into her sink and ran the water for dishes. It drowned out her voice, which was good, but he turned the tap off again abruptly.

'Super! When do you think? When? No, it's no problem. I'll shove you in Amanda's and Charlie's, or——' A pause, then a laugh. They had known each other a long time. Friends? Lovers? He pushed a small stack of plates down into the soapy water and the water surged up and sloshed over the edge of the sink. Melody said, 'I'll be waiting. Keep the pilot on course, and I'll be there to meet your plane.'

Listening to her telephone calls, wondering who meant what to her. Crazy behaviour for a grown man determined to keep control of his own life. This was beyond wanting, beyond infatuation. Too much, tentacles catching him in traps he did not want to spring.

Past time he got out of here. This afternoon he would phone and book a reservation on the next sailing of the *Queen of the North*.

CHAPTER FIVE

SHE really had to learn to keep her imagination where it belonged, in her work, Melody told herself. Crazy, but she had been feeling as if Scott had strings that would pull at her from a world away, that he was the man who could whisper her name and send her reeling, body and soul . . . today and tomorrow and forever.

Today and tomorrow and forever, words like a song. Perhaps that was it, the germ of a new song stirring in her. Not real feelings, not a frightening loss of control of mind and heart and life. Melody knew she sometimes went a little crazy when she was working. She always had. Her little bit of artistic temperament, she supposed, and no problem if she kept it inside her own head, or safely inside the soundproofed walls of the music-room. But to reach out her arms and whisper his name, to groan and feel the need to beg for his possession, surging and growing and turning wild and unchained within her——

That was madness.

Fantasy was her business, poetry. She had to learn to keep that part of her where it belonged, and Jeff's voice got her back on track. She hung up the telephone, then worked on reminding herself that Scott Alexander was a stranger, attractive and pleasant, but not touching even the surface of her life. For heaven's sake! What did she know about the man? He was Donna's brother, but she had never met Donna. He could feed a baby and change a nappy and he was a sea-captain who had to be in the Beaufort Sea in less than three weeks. Lord! She wasn't even sure where the Beaufort Sea *was*, except it was up north in the cold Arctic somewhere. And she damned well wasn't going to go running to her atlas to find out, either!

It did not matter. *He* did not matter. Not to her. He was a guest, like all the others, friends of Amanda and Charlie's, friends of Robin's. Here's your room and there's the kitchen and keep out of the music-room. Have fun, but don't bother the lady in residence.

She managed to believe it, almost, so long as she did not look too closely at Scott's eyes. Well, that was right. When had she ever watched those casual guests so closely?

She smiled at him and breezed out of the house before he could say whatever was in his eyes. She sailed through *Island Time* without thinking about him. Not much, anyway, and less all the time.

She was all right now. Unstable, but she knew that about herself. She was too easily vulnerable; needed to keep close to nature, a little isolated from the world. Here, in the space of a few days, a stranger from the wild Pacific Ocean had driven into her life with his big cross-country tyres and had turned her upside-down.

All right. So she was too easily thrown off balance, although she had not realised until the last few days that she had that kind of gasping passion buried inside her. Good for her song-writing, but best kept out of the rest of her life. She needed day following day with order, not with uncontrolled emotion. Look at the trouble she had been having with her work ever since Scott Alexander walked through her door!

She used the telephone at the radio station to call him. 'Scott? Look, I won't be able to get home for supper tonight. I've got to put in some overtime in the tape editing booth.' It was a lie. John did all the editing.

Scott's voice on the telephone told her he knew it was a lie, without words. Just undertones. Damn it! Imaginary undertones, as likely as not. Perhaps she was imagining it all, the messages in his eyes, the words unspoken and felt between them.

No matter. He was not important to her. Too dangerous.

She arrived home just before net time. She concentrated her hellos on baby Robbie, who was already drooping. She avoided talking to Scott, avoided looking at him. Then she brushed past them, the man and the baby, switching on the radio and muttering about the schedule.

She heard him going upstairs with the baby as she tuned up. It was not going to work. He was not one of the usual stream of strangers from the theatre world, invaders to be handled without actually touching them. Her people were the islanders, not the visitors, but although she had labelled him an islander at first, he was a stranger. Stranger from the sea. Stranger. Danger.

For the first time in days, the twenty-metre band was free of static. The Vancouver net control was loud and clear. She checked in, then net control called Robin's call sign. She heard her twin's voice, clear and close in her living-room. 'Melody, let's go up thirty. I'll call you.'

She shifted her frequency up thirty kilohertz and tuned in on Robin's powerful voice. His big voice was always a surprise to people who thought a slight form meant a light whisper of a voice.

'The trades are blowing twenty-five to thirty,' he told her, his voice excited. 'I've been making six knots all day.' She had been learning nautical terminology in the year since Robin dived head-first into sailing and yachting. Trade winds. A thirty-knots wind was about fifty kilometres an hour.

She felt Scott's presence behind her. She managed to keep her eyes from him, staring at the pencil in her hand, at the numbers on paper. Robin's latest position, longitude and latitude. 'Robin, when do you expect to be in Hawaii?'

She could hear the faint sound of Morse code from another amateur station, the quiet swish of Scott's shoes on her carpet, then Robin's voice saying, 'Four days, plus or minus the wind. You know how it is. No schedule out here.'

Robin had taken to the sea to escape the pressure of deadlines between appearances and recording sessions. Or had he been escaping his love for Donna, a woman who had wanted more than he could give?

What had Donna asked? That Robin give up his career, move into a house and stay in one place. That he give up his identity. Better, she thought, that Robin had resisted. Robin without music would be a pale shadow of himself.

She could feel Scott at her side. Did he expect her to tell about the baby? About Donna's death? On the radio? She keyed the microphone. 'Robin, be sure to telephone me the moment you get to shore.'

Her brother's voice snapped across the miles of ocean that separated them. 'Is Charlie's heart kicking up again?'

'No, nothing like that. It's—nothing like that. Just a snarl-up you'll have to deal with.'

Behind her, Scott moved restlessly. Angrily?

'OK,' Robin said with relief in his voice. She knew he would assume that the problem related to the upcoming recording sessions. It was forbidden to deal with business matters on amateur radio, so he said only, 'All right, Melody, if that's all, I'll sign off and go change my

Genny for the hundred per center. The wind's picking up. Eighty-eight, twin.'

Eighty-eight; love and kisses. Genny; Genoa jib sail. She smiled slightly and signed off, echoing his endearment. When Robin's voice had faded to memory, she threw the switch that brought silence flooding over the room and sat, staring at the radio, knowing she had to turn and meet Scott's eyes now. All day, she had been avoiding that.

'Why didn't you tell him?'

'On the air?' Her voice was rising as she stood up, defensive. Anger made it easier to stare at him coldly, with criticism. 'Do you know how many people are listening? Ham radio operators on several continents, not to mention the short-wave listeners! And you want me to tell him the woman he loved is dead? Flat, like that, while he's in the middle of the ocean? He'd be alone with it, out there, and I——' Her voice faltered to a gasp as she swung around to him, her hands settled on her hips and her head tossed back in preparation for battle.

The man who had fed the baby with tenderness in his eyes, that man was gone. Along with the man who had touched her, kissed her and lifted her into his arms as if his possession were total. Trapped by the harshness in his eyes, Melody felt her breath go short and her chest tighten.

Silence. Tension. 'What's wrong?' she whispered finally.

A spasm jerked across his face, then he relaxed as if he had forced the tension away. He said, 'I'm leaving on tomorrow's ferry,' and his voice held nothing more than the bare words.

'What about . . .?' She swallowed. 'You wanted to see my brother first. Robin. To be sure—to check him out.'

'I've a friend wating for me.' His jaw tensed. 'I'm supposed to be in Campbell River this week, then going on a trip with...'

To Mexico. With a friend. The woman he had telephoned? Caroline. Another sister? Girlfriend? Lover?

'Go, then,' she said, drawing all the old defences around her. Always, until Charlie and Amanda had dumped their children on the Queen Charlotte Islands, friends had been brief and transitory, here and gone; every warm contact formed had led to the pain of parting. Melody's childhood years were littered with half-memories of half-friendships, of people left behind and never seen again. As she had become older, friendships had taken longer to grow, and she had become the one on the outside. Robin had fused with the world of the stage, revelling in its excitement, but not his twin.

She had come to accept it, telling herself that it was a song-writer's lot, always being a misfit, that it was essential to the poet to view the world from the edge. Even here on her islands she was an oddity. A good place, though, for people who did not quite fit. Among the Haida, the fishermen and loggers, the island was scattered with intriguing misfits who had found a home on the misty isles where an individual was allowed to be different without penalty.

At ten years of age Melody and Robin had been thrown from their rambling backstage life into a housekeeper-supervised existence in Queen Charlotte. The islanders might have shunned the twins as outsiders, but instead they had given the newcomers the chance to prove themselves.

For Melody, the islands had become her refuge, her home, although Robin had always resented fiercely the fact that the authorities had caught up with Amanda and Charlie, insisting that two ten-year-old children could not spend their childhood without regular schooling. Robin had been singing regularly on stage that last year, while Melody had refused to join the act in front of an audience.

Now Scott nodded and said tonelessly, 'Yes, I will go. It's time. Do you need anything? Money?'

'Money?' she squeaked. 'Why should I ask for money from you? I——'

His hand caught her arm as it flung out in anger. His fingers burned her flesh through the loose knit of her sweater and he said angrily, 'For the baby. Is there anything you need for Robin Scott before I——'

'No.' The tight breathing was making her chest rise and fall visibly. Oh, lord! What had she thought he meant? He was staring at her, could see her face flaming. Her colour was always high, but now her cheeks were blazing, even her lips and her forehead, her throat. She gasped and the sound was echoed in his eyes.

She could feel the tension in him, explosive emotions boiling through her once peaceful home. It was in her, too, a violent something about to take her apart. She swallowed and jerked away, but his hand was still on her arm, burning although there was no skin contact.

'Let go of me.' The words were only a whisper. Her eyes got caught in his. The granite had changed to hazel and, as she stared into his gaze, his eyes turned dark and she forgot to breathe. She said, 'Tomorrow? You're going tomorrow?' and it was not her voice at all. Some part of her recognised the husky vulnerability that was a childhood memory of Amanda singing a love-song to Charlie on stage. She shook her head to reject the parallel and he nodded, understanding something that was not in words.

His thumb moved, calluses sliding along, catching the wool of her sweater, stirring the tender flesh at the inside of her upper arm as the heat of his moving fingers flowed through to her. He saw her swallow, saw her eyes widen and lose their focus. He was mesmerised, and his thumb stroked more gently, slipping over the barrier of her pushed-back sleeve, feeling out the softness of her forearm as his breathing paced hers. 'Tomorrow,' he echoed as her lips parted unconsciously. 'Or now,' he growled, and he was closer, his eyes on her lips, on the soft smoothness of her long neck, the trembling at the base of her throat.

She managed to say shakily, 'Now would be better. Go now.' Far better. This was dangerous, playing with explosive unknowns. She could get badly burned if she let herself drown in this trembling vulnerability. She might drown, never to find herself again. She told her arm to pull away, but his fingers slid down and his thumb found her inner wrist. The caress shot right through her but she managed to turn her groan into words, to whispers. 'Scott, I—please, I want you to go away now.'

His lips were closer. Her tongue slipped out to moisten her own swollen, dry lips and her teeth caught her lower lip.

He did not smile, just stared at her in the reddish glow that was the sun setting outside, draining light from the world. He lifted her hand and bent his mouth, not to her lips, but to her inner wrist.

She felt the trembling in her knees, the weakness, but she would not give in to the soft agony of his lips, his tongue playing along her pulse. Her fingers clenched on nothing. He felt the movement and whispered, 'If you want me to go, you'd better decide. Now.'

'Yes,' she gasped, but his tongue did not stop its erotic journey along the nerves of her inner arm, her wrist, the curve of her palm. As his lips moved, his eyes traced the motion of her breathing, finding the full swelling of her breasts under the oversized sweater. What if he touched there? His lips moved back to her wrist, towards her elbow, but his eyes were everywhere and she could feel the reaction in her body, tightening and aching. 'Go,' she gasped. 'Please go.'

He was not even holding her in his arms. What if he did? He was a foot or so away, the only contact his fingers on her wrist, his mouth along her forearm. And she could feel the hunger swelling inside herself. Her legs did not want to hold her. If she sagged closer he would touch and hold and take over what would happen. 'Go,' she whispered again, wanting him to pull her into his arms and end the tension.

He dropped her wrist. She stood motionless, vulnerable and exposed, because he could see and she could not seem to cover up what he was taking from her eyes. He raised one hand and slowly brought it to her. She could feel the movement of the air, herself shivering as his fingers slowly found the front of her sweater. She could feel herself tightening, and when his fingers stroked lightly over the peaks of her breasts through the wool, the hard buds of her nipples were so achingly sensitive with waiting, needing, knowing the touch would come, that she groaned aloud, choking the sound to a gulp and silence.

'Please,' she whispered.

He pulled his hand back, but his voice was seduction overlaid with a low anger. 'I don't ravish youngsters, music lady, and you're no child, so make up your mind.' His eyes found the thrust of her aroused breasts, telling her without words that he knew she wanted his touch.

'I don't understand what you mean,' she whispered, confused.

He shook his head. She felt the tension break when he turned away. She sagged down on to the carpet, staring at the fire as he moved around her room. She did not watch him, but the flames. He was moving, pacing. In a minute there would be his footsteps on the stairs. Why could he not let her play the harmless game of self-deception? She could say *go*, and he would touch her, kiss her, and somehow despite her protests he would make love to her before he walked away. Oh, God! She ached for his touch, but so much better if she said no even though she trembled for him, because she would have herself intact later. A night's passion, but not of her asking.

Love.

If she turned and looked at him, whispered a word of consent, it would happen. An affair, hot and quick and over. If it happened now, in the morning he would leave, or perhaps even earlier. He was a stranger, a sailor who had come and would go, and she knew almost nothing of him, except that he was tender with the baby, and that he was not a man for staying. And he would not take her and sweep her away on a tide of passion, not without making sure first that she was just as responsible as him.

Lover. A lover, for a night. Temporary. She tried to put the words into her mind, but although she knew he would walk away, his soul touched hers when their eyes met.

The music released her. Had he known it would? How much did he know? How far past her barriers could he see? She turned and the yellow flames from the fire were still in her eyes, but he was there, at the stereo, and the music was flowing over them both. Her own words, flowing over her mind, with meaning they had not had when she'd written them two years ago. 'Touch of a stranger, a lover's touch. Two souls meeting before they part.'

She did not look away, could not look away. He moved slowly, deliberately, crossing from the stereo to the fireplace where she sat on the thick carpet. Her hand moved and she saw it stretch towards him, but he passed her. He went to the fire and shifted a log, sending sparks blazing around. When he turned back to her he was all hardness and control.

She swallowed and her lips parted, but the words were somewhere else.

He said softly, 'Melody, do you want me to go away? Now?'

She shook her head, wordless. The door would close and the truck would drive down her tortured hill. She would have to go out and move her van to let him out, and she would be shivering, watching the red of his taillights as he drove away. Forever.

They would meet again. Around the baby. Over the years. But there would never be this, because whatever happened tonight would be isolated, a memory only. She did not dare let Scott be a part of her life; he could consume her.

He stroked the dark hair away from her cheek, his fingers curling around the full curve of her cheekbones. 'If I stay,' he said intently, his eyes on hers, 'you know what's going to happen.'

If he walked away now, she would never know what her own songs were about. Dreams, she had thought, writing them, but the dreams were here, now, in his eyes and her veins. She curled her fingers around his wrist and felt his pulse beating, strong and hard. And she said, 'Don't go. Not yet.'

It was like a song. The music. The magic. The slow dance of reality and anticipation. He sank down slowly beside her, not touching, only eyes, and she felt her lips curving in a smile as she turned towards him. The smile and the movement and the anticipation of his touch were all dreaming. His eyes followed the curves of her body and she realised that the sweater that covered everything, covered nothing.

She licked her lips and he touched them with his, pulling back to see her eyes. What did he want her to be? She saw his chest swell beneath the brown shirt he wore as he took in a deep, powerful breath. Her fingers curled, wanting to touch.

'Touch me. Touch my soul.' Words, a song, flowing over them. His fingers reached her shoulder and stroked her arm through the sweater, a teasing hint of later, of how his touch would be on her naked flesh. Her hand moved between them and she traced the contours of his hard chest.

He took her mouth. The music exploded.

She had needed this, had ached for him. His lips covered hers, and she opened to him, invited his invasion of her warm, moist mouth, shuddered and groaned soundlessly as her body flowed against his, his hands holding her arms, bringing her close, his arms surrounding her. A safe...warm...hot nest where there was only warmth and touch and feeling and the surging of the music felt in their veins.

Her breasts pushed hard against his chest. His hands spread out to span her back, fingers touching to make flames along her nerves. Her spine arched and he moulded her fine-boned torso to his hard muscles. She gasped as one hand slipped under her sweater and his fingers traced up her spine with sensuous, soft abrasion.

When he lifted his lips from hers, she found herself staring up at him, lying on her back on the soft plush carpet. Behind him, she could see the red brilliance of the sun's last glow, the sunset surrounding his head like a halo of fire. Longer days, she thought. Summer coming soon. Then she could think of nothing but him.

He said, 'I want to see you,' and she needed his eyes on her with the touch of a lover.

She stroked the crispness of his shirt, found the place between two buttons and slipped her fingers through, into the rough curls of his chest hair.

He growled, 'If you do that . . .' and she laughed, her voice husky and teasing and drowned out by the song. 'Touching. Loving. Your mind caressing mine.'

'Touch me,' she whispered, and his eyes turned to flames. His hands traced the shape of her, through the clothing, and she was naked while fully clothed, shuddering, feeling his caress everywhere. His hands settled under her breasts, curving to hold them, and she gasped, 'Please.'

'Don't be impatient.' He gave a low laugh, stroking her midriff, the sweater transmitting his message. Her eyes fell shut and there was only the soft teasing of his hands everywhere, and her fingers worrying at his buttons, her groan as he stroked her thigh through the jeans, her swollen breast through bra and sweater, her hip.

Then stillness. Her eyes dragged open. She had found her way through the buttons, or he had. His shirt was gaping open, her hands threading through the hair, finding the hard curve of his male breast, the arousal of his tiny nipples, the rigid tension of his upper abdomen. His fingers were resting on the naked flesh of her midriff, under the sweater, but motionless. In a second he would move, the sweater would be gone, then everything else, and she would go up in fire, consumed.

'Melody, are you prepared for this?'

She stared at him. His fingers moved, so slightly, and her flesh shuddered. Prepared? She was aching for him, needing him with a drugging, wild passion that had come from somewhere inside, from the place where the songs came, the secret, mysterious, all-consuming hidden part of her.

'Yes,' she whispered, because she had been waiting all her life for his touch on her soul. 'Please touch me.'

It was more than she had thought it could be, so much more. He pushed up the sweater, so slowly, and his eyes aroused her long before his hands and lips could touch. She writhed with impatience, with need, and the sweater was gone.

He cupped her breasts with love, and bent to the sweet curve that he had pushed up from her bra, his lips and his breath hot on her. Then he freed her of the scrap of lace with an abrupt motion and took his freedom of her warmth with his lips.

She would go mad with the sensations. Touching, fire, the song in her ears and her blood and the pounding of her wild heart. She twisted, writhed, told him with formless sounds how she needed the feel of his lips and his hands and his body on hers, while her own hands roamed over his chest and his shoulders with restless seduction.

'I've dreamed of you like this,' he groaned as he freed her of the last trace of clothing, as he bent to take the place of the flames playing light over her softly glowing flesh. The rough hair of his leg invaded the softness of her inner thighs and she moved to reach for his possession of her. 'Loving you,' he whispered, tracing fingers over the curve of her belly. 'Touching,' he breathed, and his lips moved to the places his hands had been. 'I dreamed of you needing me the way I burn for you,' he said harshly as she pulled him closer.

She rose to meet him and he filled her as the rain fills the river, the thunder invading the mountains with gasping rightness. His need was hers, and when she groaned, he shuddered with an echoing passion that grew to consume them both. Then the music was gone and the sun was gone, and there was only the explosion of the stars, the earth shifting, torn out of its orbit as she fell spinning into the place where there was no Melody, no Scott, only the soft, hot, wild, hard demand that was their shuddering fulfilment.

She lay very still, listening to the beating of his heart under her cheek. Slowly, the wild pounding calmed to a steady, strong thump. She wanted to lift her head and turn to see his face, but he was quiet, motionless, holding her, and she felt the words that he was not saying.

If she opened her eyes and looked into his, would he see how much he had taken from her? More than passion. She squeezed her eyelids tightly closed and held her body carefully relaxed. In her throat, words were welling up. Stay. Please. Don't leave me. Don't go away. Not today. Not tomorrow.

The music had stopped, but her mind played back the final song of the album, knowing those notes must have filled the dark room only moments ago, and that she had been too drowned in Scott to hear.

Instant replay, she thought, trying to feel cool and a little scornful of her own desire to reach and cling and whisper words of love and need. She opened her eyes without turning to see his face, keeping very still. His chest hairs, in front of her face, curled damply across his male breast. Behind him, the fire burned, low now, except for the occasional burst of blue flame as flames consumed sap on the wood.

She felt tension in his still body. He was waiting for her to sleep. She understood that, shared the unwillingness to speak or look. They had gone farther, come closer than either of them could handle. The knowledge hurt, and she knew that the dreams and the memories were going to hurt, too. The sight of him over the years to come was going to stir pain and longing inside her, because this could never happen again. She could not handle it without begging for more, for closeness and sharing and a relationship.

That kind of needing scared her silly. For three years she had been her own person, *needed* to be her own person. She must not let herself be swallowed up in emotion, passion, needing.

Not that she was at risk. Scott was going to run, too, just as soon as he thought she was asleep. All right. Better that way. The next time she saw him he would be a stranger again, the baby's uncle, and she would be safe back in her own world, insulated from the storm he had woken in her. She would dress very carefully, put on make-up and a cool smile, and he would never see anything but the well-groomed shell of her public self.

Scott looked in on Robbie after he had his things packed in the bag. The baby was just stirring, grumbling sleepily that it was time for his night feed. Best if he walked away and let Melody wake to tend the baby, but he picked Robbie up and took him into the kitchen. He forced himself not to look at Melody as he carried the baby past, but he saw her, lying nestled under the quilt he had brought down to cover her.

She was lying on her stomach, her face pillowed by her forearm. Her long, black eyelashes were fanned over her full cheeks. Even in sleep, with her normally sleek hair tumbled by the passion of their loving, she looked fresh and beautiful. None of her dramatic colouring was artifice.

He heated the bottle, fed Robbie, then burped him and changed him and put him back into the playpen upstairs. He stared down at the baby, feeling guilty in the knowledge that he was about to walk out on his young nephew. But he had to go. Self-preservation.

He had never met anyone like her before. The dreamy passion of her songs was there in her eyes, peeking through the barrier of her mask. He had sensed it from the first, had wanted her from the beginning.

She had been more than he expected, had touched him in places both moving and terrifying. Melody Connacher. Dangerous Melody. She looked so smooth and sophisticated, so carefully groomed, even in that sloppy sweater she wore. Controlled on the outside, with eyes exposing the emotional woman underneath. High colour in her cheeks. Eyes that went black with emotion. Body that curved to hold and comfort a small child. Lord! He had started dreaming about her! Then the dreams had burst the bounds of his sleeping fantasies.

Dreaming. And doing things for her. It had started out as the old, learned habit of his childhood, because he had known that she did not want him here, and he had felt a stubborn determination to stay.

Thrown into foster-homes when his parents died, Scott had learned quickly that while his two-year-old sister Donna was cute and cuddly, eight-year-old Scott was awkward and difficult. Donna could smile and gurgle and win anyone over. Scott had known, even at the age of eight, that he could not win his place in strange homes with a smile. Instead, he had worked quietly, looking for the jobs that needed doing, trying to make himself indispensable. The dishes. The rubbish. Chopping wood.

It had worked for three years, until their foster-mother had discovered she was pregnant and pushed away both Donna and Scott in favour of her natural child. When they were placed together again with a fisherman and his wife, Scott had vowed to make himself completely indispensable this time.

That was how it had started with Melody, he supposed. The old habit, quietly looking for tasks to do to compensate for his unwelcome presence. Then it had got out of hand, and he had fallen into the pattern of protecting her working time, sharing Robbie with her, sharing moments in the evening with her, lunches and cups of coffee, moments of listening to music.

Insane though it was, he had begun to think of this place as if it were his own home. Had begun to think of the woman as if she were his. That was the frightening part, because he had vowed years ago that he was never going to let anyone get close enough to tear his life apart by walking away. Never again. A child had little choice, but a man could choose his life.

Choose his women. Far better to have a woman like Caroline, cool and independent and more concerned with her own career than with their relationship. That was how he wanted it.

He stopped on his way out of the house, stood in the darkened living-room and stared down at Melody's dark curls. He caught himself before he actually reached down to touch her. If he touched, stroked, whispered her name, she would murmur and sigh and finally turn to him, open her arms to him and make him whole again.

Angrily, he broke away from her spell. Soft trap. How could a man possess her complexities? Song-writer. Semi-recluse. Hot, passionate lover. If he didn't get away quickly, she would have a stranglehold on his soul. She would have him begging for the moon, then she would drift out of his arms with a few words of poetry. He didn't need risks like that. A life of turning on the radio and hearing her words, dreaming of her with dreams he could not escape.

He managed to get the truck out without driving on the soft part of her lawn. He couldn't avoid leaving tracks on the edge of the grass, but he thought the grass would spring back if he raked it. He stopped the truck at the top of the twisting drop and pulled on the emergency brake. It would only take a minute to get her rake from the shed behind the house.

Get the hell out of here, before it's too late!

He had the door half-open, but he jerked it shut. The slam of metal on metal burst the quiet of the night. He clenched his jaw and forced his actions to slow. Then he let the brake off and eased his way down the hill.

Sneaking away, his heart pounding with turmoil. God! Here he was, thirty-six years old, and he felt the way he had when he was fifteen, after that big blow-up with Tom, his second foster-father. Scott had been kicked out of high school for continuous truancy, and Tom had laid the law down. School, or work, or get the hell out. Tom, accustomed to the harsh life of a fisherman, had enforced his anger with blows, and Scott had run when he'd caught himself about to strike back.

That night he'd been on foot, roaming Vancouver's streets, not driving a big, powerful truck along a winding island highway. Steamed up, angry, frightened and too foolish to admit it. He had moved from the respectable area into the wild, and somewhere in the angry night he had begun to see what was around him. Homeless people. Old men without families; girls pretending to be women, selling what should only be given with love.

Inside the houses, safe and secluded were the families. Scott had had no family except Donna, and his sister had been clinging to Tom and Sylvia so hard that she had hardly seemed to remember Scott was her brother.

He had felt cut off, isolated by the anger of the man he could not bring himself to call *father*. Then, somewhere between the drunk asleep in the alley, and the girl on the street who looked so much like Donna, he had lost the anger and realised that, no matter how alone he felt as a barely tolerated foster-child, it was nothing to the isolation of having no one.

In the morning, when Tom had arrived at the *Lady Sylvia*, Scott had been waiting. They had stared at each other. If Tom had said anything about the night before, Scott would have gone. Perhaps Tom realised that, because his face had worked silently, then he had nodded abruptly and said, 'Sandpaper in the wheelhouse. We're stripping down the gunwales to paint them.'

That stormy night had been over twenty years ago. Tom had never been his father, but after that night they had developed a restrained relationship that had worked. Perhaps by the time the old fisherman died they had become friends of a sort.

Turning back had been the right choice then, but tonight was different, the risks the other way, and safety was in getting away before he got in over his head. So he drove, instinctively putting miles between himself and Melody. He followed the only highway there was, the winding, narrow route north along the east coast of Graham Island. He had a lot of time to kill. The ferry that would take him away was not scheduled to leave until midnight. He had the dawn to wait for, then a full day.

He stopped at a stream beside the road, cupped his hands and filled them with cool mountain water. The water tasted of pine. There was a sign posted at the edge of the clearing where he had pulled off the road. He read the legend and learned that anyone who drank the waters of St Mary's Spring would always return to the Misty Isles.

He felt a sudden, irrational terror, as if the legend were another strand pulling him down into quicksand. He slammed into the truck and drove on and managed to talk sense to his crazy imagination. All right. Of course he would come back. For Robbie, his nephew. He would come back and visit, take his nephew out for fishing trips.

Would Robbie live here? Did Robin Conners actually live in the Queen Charlotte house, or was it merely a place he visited? Did Melody live alone with her music and her dreams? The music-room seemed to belong so totally to her that he had trouble imagining her sharing it with anyone else.

Were there men? Jeff, for instance? The man who had telephoned and seemed to know her habits so intimately. Would Scott come to visit Robbie, and find her with another man? Any man would want her, and this Jeff probably did. A woman like Melody, filled with warmth and dreams——

One day he would come back and she would be married. Another man's child would lie in her arms, nuzzling against her breast for comfort and food.

A car came at him, then swerved. Then the haze in front of Scott cleared and he saw the yellow line on his right. He was on the wrong side of the road! He jerked the wheel and the car flashed by, horn blasting in a wail of frightened protest.

He pulled off the road, still shaking from the close call. He could have killed the innocent driver of that car! He had to get control of himself, stop painting pictures of Melody on the telephone with a man named Jeff. Smiling and laughing. Excited.

Melody, her head thrown back, her mouth open on a gasp as Scott touched her throat with his lips. Melody, soft and wild under him, her skin glowing with firelight as he possessed her. His name, whispered on the night air. Melody's whisper.

CHAPTER SIX

MELODY wanted to go to Hawaii to meet Robin, but she hesitated to take the baby with her. Scott had had trouble with Robbie on the ferry. If the baby got seasick, he might well get airsick, too.

Scott. When would his name on her mind turn to something ordinary, instead of leaving her with this trembling emptiness?

Melody wanted to meet Robin in Hawaii, but could not accept the idea of leaving Robbie behind with Mrs Winston. The housekeeper had not been very much of a mother substitute for Melody and Robin. Maybe Robbie was too small to notice, but he had already lost his mother. He needed stability.

But to tell Robin about Donna's death on the telephone——

The baby started screaming just before noon the day after Scott left. Melody realised that her concept of time was changing, that life was organised into 'before Scott came', 'when Scott was here', and 'after Scott left'. He was the lover in her dreams, in her songs.

Jeff turned up just as Robbie started screaming.

'You drive,' she said as he walked through the door. 'To the hospital.'

He looked startled, but recovered quickly. 'Yes, ma'am,' he said and he got her there quickly.

The problem was diagnosed quickly. A night in the hospital and she had Robbie back, but with the caution, 'He's got a hernia in his groin. It's slipped back into place now, but watch him. It may have to be operated on, but we'd like to wait until he's at least a month older.'

Robin called the next night, the telephone ringing in the middle of the night. Melody stumbled downstairs to grab it before it woke the baby, Jeff, in the room that had been Scott's, slept through the noise.

Her twin's voice was vibrant over the miles. 'What is it? Don't tell me they've messed up on the dates for the recording studio.'

'You're in Hawaii?' Why had she not practised the words, ways to tell him. 'Do you know what time it is here? When did you get in?' *Donna's dead. The woman you loved is gone.*

'Just now.' He was laughing at her confusion, not repentant for interrupting her sleep. 'Just cleared Customs now and got my cruising permit. What's up, Melody?'

In the end she said it bluntly, because she knew no soft way. She blurted, 'Donna Alexander's dead.'

Nothing. He did not say a word. She gripped the receiver, wished she could touch him, see him. How could she have broken the news to him so brutally?

'Oh, God,' he whispered. 'No. Please, no.'

'Robin, there's a baby. Your baby.'

He did not hear. He whispered, 'Donna——'

She remembered when they had been twelve years old and he had tried to keep a trapped squirrel in captivity. It had died. She remembered Robin's face, his eyes just before he had stormed out of the house. He had been gone six days. Everyone had searched. Mrs Winston. The police. Even Amanda and Charlie, called home from a nightclub engagement in France.

She gripped the receiver tighter. 'Robin? I—look, what city are you in? Where in Hawaii? What marina? I'll come there. I——'

'No!' He sounded angry, but she knew it was not anger.

'Robin! Listen to me! Don't go off and—— The baby—the baby needs you. Your baby. Donna's——'

There was a choked sound, then nothing but the hollow sound of her own telephone.

She hung up quickly, hoping that he would call back, knowing he would not. He needed time. Why was it that they could never share their worst hurts with each other?

'Don't worry,' she told the baby softly as she fed him. 'He'll come. And...even if he doesn't, I'll look after you.'

Jeff knew nothing about babies and had no intention of learning, despite Melody's threat that she would tell his next girlfriend what a rotten baby-sitter he was. So Melody got Mrs Winston to baby-sit while she was away at the radio station. On Monday she went through *Island Time* in a fog, but on Tuesday she got hold of herself, and by Thursday she managed most of her time on the air without thinking about Scott.

Jeff made up for his inadequacy as a baby-sitter by overhauling her synthesiser while she was at the station, getting rid of an annoying buzz tht occurred whenever she tried to lay a percussion track over bass guitar. What he didn't know about synthesisers hadn't been discovered yet.

He was the kind of guest she had always liked. If he was hungry, he fed himself or went out to a restaurant. When he wasn't playing with her equipment he was reading, technical magazines and horror novels alternately. When she was restless and unable to work, he talked her into getting Mrs Winston for the evening and going out dancing at the hotel.

But Scott was haunting her daydreams, giving her nightmares. She was fighting a losing battle in trying to talk herself out of the infatuation. It had been too long since she had taken a romantic interest in a man. She had been too long in an emotional vacuum, with only the fantasies in her music-room. It hadn't been Scott, but her own needs exploding. It could have been any attractive man.

She did not believe her own arguments. There were attractive men all around her. Jeff was attractive, although she had never felt anything but comradeship with Jeff. There was a man in the advertising department at the radio station, too, tall and handsome and single, and he left her cold.

She was in limbo, unable to work or to think straight. She told herself it was Robin she was waiting for. He would call, or he would come, and until then she could not make any plans for her future. She wasn't sure why she had to plan, but she felt a desperate need for something to hang on to.

She stumbled through the days. Reality was the hours in the sound-room, letting her feelings loose on the music. Reality was holding Robbie in her arms. Everything else was a haze, but she had control. At the radio station, she made her voice light and warm and friendly. At home, she tended to Robbie's needs, fed him and changed him and sang to him. She listened to Jeff talking, nodded and murmured to keep his words flowing.

Would Robin never call, never come? Two weeks, now three? Three weeks, Scott had said. That was the day he brought Robbie to her. Three weeks and he had to be on board his ship. The days had passed and she had counted. Scott would be there now, on his ship, and she had only a hazy picture of a formless ship in the midst of the ice, Scott at the bridge.

She wished Jeff would go so that she could stop pretending to be cheerful. Then, suddenly, he did leave, and it was worse, because she had no one now to distract her from her thoughts.

Before Jeff left, he caught her chin with his long fingers and tipped her face up, examining it carefully. 'Want to talk about it?' he asked.

She shook her head. She should have known Jeff would see that she was disturbed, but talking about it would only make it seem more real. Infatuation. Not love. It would go away if she tried hard enough, waited long enough.

He said simply, 'If you do, you know how to find me.'

'I know. Thanks,' she whispered.

He kissed her cheek and was gone, leaving her alone with Robbie and her worries about Robin, her memories of Scott.

Mrs Winston left for a holiday in Vancouver with her husband, so Melody took the baby with her, playpen and all, to the radio station. Scott would not like that. She shrugged away that thought angrily, but the next day she got Bev to look after Robbie. Robin Scott. Donna had named her baby after the two most important men in her life, her lover and her brother. For Melody, it meant that every time she said the baby's name she would be haunted.

Once a week, everyone on board the *Jonathan Cartier*, from the messman to the skipper, had a chance to make a five-minute telephone call home.

Last year and the year before Scott had used the single weekly call to phone Sylvia, his foster-mother, because he had made himself responsible for her since Tom's death. Sometimes last year Donna had been there, as if she needed that small symbol of family, talking to her brother, although at that time he'd had no idea she was expecting a lover's child. She'd been bright and independent, talking about her job at the medical clinic, her plans to redecorate her apartment.

This year Donna was gone, and Sylvia had confided that telephone calls flustered her, that she would rather have a short visit when he got his two weeks off. So Scott had left the company's number with a neighbour, eliciting a promise to send an emergency message if Sylvia seemed to need anything. Then he had made a quick trip back to the Gorge and checked that everything on his property was secure for his six-week absence.

He'd told himself that life would be simpler on the ship this year. No one to call, so he needn't bother with the hassle of riding the man-basket to the rig, of dressing up for the cold for just five minutes on the telephone.

He supposed he could call Caroline, but he had never called her from the ship before. She would be startled by a satellite telephone call, might wonder if he was trying to deepen their relationship. Relationship? That was a laugh after the fiasco of this last month.

He had fled Queen Charlotte, arriving in Campbell River in time to go on the promised holiday to Mexico with Caroline. Then, abruptly, he'd changed his mind at the last second. She'd shouted at him at the airport and he really did not blame her. If he was going to let her down, he could have done it earlier, in time for her to make other plans. As it was, she'd stormed through the security check-point, boarded the jet without him. And he had been glad to see her go.

He had taken the ferry to his property on Gorge harbour and spent two weeks of furious activity that put his construction schedule ahead by a month, but did nothing to erase Melody Connacher from his dreams.

He would not be surprised to go on his next leave and find that there was no Caroline in his life. He knew that it would be a relief if she dumped him. He had no business holding on to her in a cool, no-future relationship, especially not now that he could not think of touching a woman, even talking to one, without fantasies of a beautiful recluse on the misty isles.

And how the hell was he going to forget Melody when he had been stupid enough to have brought Donna's stereo walkman to the Beaufort with him, and all her Robin Conners tapes? Robin Conners, singing love-songs written by his sister. Love-songs making hot dreams in the cold Arctic.

The Beaufort. Secretly he'd always found it romantically remote. He had never before felt that he was flying off to nowhere. First the airline flight to Calgary, then the company jet to Tuktoyaktuk. Then the helicopter. Huddling in the shed at Tuk, taking off his boots and pulling on the survival suit for the helicopter trip. The suit had built-in boots, hood, mitts, and he'd always felt a sense of adventure, setting off into the ice fields, always enjoyed the cold air biting into his lungs as he ran out to the chopper, carrying his kit and his boots.

But this time the hour-long flight to the rig seemed like a journey to the end of the world, cut off from the warmth, from Melody.

He had resisted the urge to pick up a telephone and call her all through those two weeks at the Gorge. But as the chopper touched down on the rig he felt a desperate need to reassure himself that she was all right, that her voice still had its husky, warm tones.

Or was he fooling himself? She would be fine, of course she would. What he needed was to know that she was not in the arms of the man named Jeff. Scott angrily shoved the jealous thought aside.

He stumbled out on to the rig. It was colder, the ice biting into him as he breathed, wind driving the effective temperature down. He glanced at the ice-pack on the horizon as he dodged into another little shed, absently assessing it as one-tenth ice, perhaps two-tenths. Around the rig, of course, the ice had been cleared.

With the return to work, the details filled the place Melody had invaded. He absorbed the mood of the men around him, knew that there was no emergency, that today everything was going smoothly. He took off the helicopter survival suit, and handed it to Cal, the skipper he would be relieving.

'Bloody freezing today,' said Cal, as he always did.

'Not much warmer in Tuk,' said Scott.

'Don't know why I work in the Arctic,' muttered the older Master. 'I'm going to Acapulco, sit in the sun while you freeze your toes, and you'll be lucky if I'm here to relieve you next time.'

'I'll dream about you,' said Scott, grinning, but it was Melody who would fill his dreams. Cal put on the helicopter suit and Scott put on the anti-exposure coveralls that would float a man if he went overboard, and keep him alive if the water weren't quite so cold. Scott had no intention of falling in and trying it out, not in those waters.

Details took over. He shoved his pack into the net of the man-basket, caught hold of the net high up and stepped on to the wide ledge at the bottom. Then he nodded and the crane operator lifted him, swinging the basket out over the icebreaker alongside the rig. It was a routine task; the crane operator halted the swing and Scott gripped the net, leaning into the basket while it swung high over his ship. Then the operator released the brake and the basket slid downwards, settling on to the deck of the icebreaker *Jonathan Cartier*.

Details. Work. A problem with the starboard bow thrusters. Parts flown in by chopper. Ice maps studied each time they came in on the fax from Ice Central. This early in the season, the ice was still heavier than he liked. He watched the drift of the pack, the forecasts of the movement of ice. They all watched, the officers of the rig and the two supply ships. A change in the pack, ice drifting down on the rig, and the routine of their days could turn into a desperate race to get the rig out before the ice took over.

She was in his dreams, but he thought he had control of it. It was a complete surprise to him on the second Wednesday evening when he turned to the mate and said, 'I'll go across for my phone call first. Then you and the second mate can go while I man the bridge.'

Harry nodded, automatically accepting the Skipper's right to first go at the telephone. It was Scott who asked himself who the hell he was going to call, and knew the answer.

Jonathan Cartier was anchored off the starboard side of the rig, backed up on her anchor with lines on to the rig. An hour earlier the chopper had landed, bringing the relief second and third engineer and two seamen, and taking away four men for their weeks off. The chopper had brought supplies, too, groceries for the rig and the icebreaker, as well as the smaller supply ship. Harry, an avid movie-watcher, was excited because the chopper had brought new movies for the men to watch during quiet evenings.

Once the chopper was gone, and the supplies transferred, the icebreaker stayed in her position, half-moored against the rig. Scott rode across, his head tipped back and watching the cable, something he never did. The cables were tested regularly. A man was crazy to get up in the air clinging to an upside-down cone at the end of a wire, and then start thinking about the wire breaking, about things that would prevent him ever seeing a certain woman again.

He had never had a serious affair with a woman. Friends, yes. Romantic friendships, like his long-standing relationship with Caroline, but never a woman who had had the power to make him yearn for her when he was far away. It scared him, frightened him even more now that he was going to call her, and did not know what he would say when her voice came.

The radio operator on the rig was just about to put the call through when head office came on with a long message that sounded far too routine to take priority over Melody, but the personal phone calls always took second place to company business.

Then, too soon, the radio op nodded and Scott went into the little room where there was a chair and a telephone and nothing much else. Thank God he had privacy at least. If he sounded like an idiot, no one would hear but himself and Melody, and any enthusiastic short-wave listener who had a fetish for tuning in on satellite telephone conversations. He had no idea what he would say to her. He had never had any trouble talking to a woman before, probably because none of them had mattered very much. Now he felt as if every word he might say would be wrong, either too clumsy or too revealing.

What the hell did he want, anyway? Her face swam in front of his eyes and he tried to put his hunger into rational words to reassure himself. An affair? The kind of relationship he had enjoyed with Caroline?

Her voice sounded warm and clear. Very close.

'Scott?' He thought he heard her draw in a breath, like a gasp, but then it was gone and she said briskly, 'I thought you'd be in the far north by now.'

'I am.'

She gave a half-laugh, and he could see how her face would be, arrested, listening, a little startled. 'You have pay phones up there?' she asked, not believing it.

'No, it's a satellite system on the oil rig.' He caught himself on the verge of explaining the technical aspects of the system. He had five minutes, for God's sake! 'It— we get to make personal calls once a week.' He heard himself saying it that way, *calls*, knew he was not ready to tell her that she was the only person he wanted to talk to. He added quickly, 'How's Robbie?'

'Oh—of course, he's fine.' He heard a rustle and she said, 'He's here. I'm just burping him.'

He saw her, clearly, saw the tenderness on her face as she looked down at the baby. Then she spoke and he realised that he was sitting here, silent, saying nothing like a fool.

'What did you want?' she asked, then interrupted herself. 'Oh, Robbie, of course. You—you sound as if you're right next door. I—did you have fun in Mexico?'

'Change of plans,' he said abruptly. 'How are you? How's——?'

Her voice seemed brittle. A distortion from the satellite, or she was not comfortable talking to him. She said, 'Robbie's got a little hernia. The doctor says it might have to be operated on, but——'

That was why she sounded so odd. Not that she was remembering their last night with discomfort, wishing it had never happened. She was concerned about the baby. Scott breathed again and said, 'Where is he? In the hospital? I'll——'

'No. It's really not serious. The doctor says it's pretty common, and the baby's not in any pain. Just——'

'Do you want me to come?'

He was working out a radio message to the company for emergency leave when she finally answered, 'You can't, can you? Your ship needs you, and all that. And why should you? It's nothing serious.'

'He's my nephew, Melody. I'm not going to just fade away to nothing.'

She said tightly. 'You did. You disappeared in the— in the night, without a word.'

'It seemed the best thing. Melody——' If only he could see her, have some feeling for what she might be thinking. He felt uncomfortably aware that his time must be almost up. 'Melody, I can be there in less than twenty-four hours. If you need me, I——'

'I don't.'

All right. She didn't. He was the one having dreams, fantasies he didn't want, couldn't shake. He amended it to, 'If Robin needs me.' He told her how to get a message to him, then asked, 'What about your brother? Is he there?' What about Jeff? Who the hell was Jeff, anyway?

'Any day now. He called from Hawaii.'

Scott frowned. What was she not telling him? Her voice had tensed and he knew something was wrong. 'Isn't he behind schedule? He should be there by now, there in Queen Charlotte with you.'

'He's . . . delayed.'

He heard the knock on the door then. Five minutes gone. Melody gone, out of his reach for seven days, until he could call again.

She waited by the telephone the next Wednesday. He had not said he would call, but he had said phone calls once a week, and it was a Wednesday when he called before. She spent the whole week telling herself she didn't care if he called, except for when Robin came home and she really did manage to forget about Scott for a while.

At first Melody had thought Robin was reaching for his baby only because it was the child of the woman he had loved. If so, the infant soon wound its own spell over the man.

'I'm going to find a house,' he told Melody, young Robbie held against his shoulder for a burp. 'Come on, Robbie. One big burp for your dad. Not an elaborate house, though. Something that feels like home. Like this.'

'There's this house,' offered Melody. She watched the father and son, seeing Robin's dark eyes echoed in his child, his slight, fine-boned figure. She could share the work of bringing the baby up. 'It's as much yours as mine, and there's surely room. And jets to LA, you can make connection in Vancouver. You could——'

He shook his head, not smiling now. 'No, my dear twin. This is your haven, but it's not mine. I like these islands, but I probably wouldn't come back at all if it weren't that you were here, making this place feel like a home. If I lived here with Robbie, you know how it would be.'

He frowned at his son and said sombrely, 'She wouldn't marry me, you see, because she was certain that a performer couldn't make a home. That I'd be off and away all the time, always leaving her, and she'd be more lonely with me than without. I told her—I promised her that I wouldn't let it be like that. That we could make a home, a real home, even though I had to travel to perform. But she needed a home, you see. She'd lost her parents before she could remember, been a foster-child, had a foster-father who was always at sea.'

Melody did not know what to say. She thought she understood how poor Donna must have felt. Robin was so passionate, so effervescent, and so impulsive. A woman might worry that he would chain her, and then disappear.

Scott would have shared Donna's childhood. If it had made Donna insecure, it seemed to have made Scott strong. Had it also made him wary of loving and families?

Robin said, 'I promised her. She didn't believe me, that it could work, but—— Our child will have the home I would have given her if she'd lived.' He blinked, hard, and his jaw went rigid. Melody knew he did not want her sympathy to erode his self-control.

He said, 'Somewhere near Los Angeles, I think. Or at least somewhere close to a major airport where I can get to LA in a couple of hours. I'll find a housekeeper. Someone who's good with kids.' A wife was what he needed, she thought, but with the shadow of Donna in his eyes she could not say so.

He said, 'I'll be there every night I can.' He caught her eyes and held them. 'Melody, I'm not going to keep Robbie here. You know what would happen. I'd take advantage of you. You'd tie up the rest of your life with my child. It's time you reached out for your own life. I'm not going to give you excuses to hide away.'

What would he think if she told him that her life was growing its own complexities? People talked about twins' lives running in parallel, but this was ridiculous! Robin, with a child he had unknowingly fathered. And Melody——

'I've got two weeks,' he said, moving away with Robbie. 'I'm going to put Robbie to bed and——'

'For two weeks?' She had missed something here.

He smiled. 'No, idiot. For a nap. Then I'll get on the phone and organise things. Get estate agents looking, get something fixed up temporarily. I'll take Robbie to LA with me, to my apartment, and get someone to look after him while I'm working.'

She said, 'The studio's booked a week from now.'

'Practice sessions. Robbie can come to them.' He grinned and she laughed, thinking it a good thing that she had been taking the baby into her music-room, getting him used to the sounds. He added, 'Not to the recording sessions.'

The twins stared at each other silently across the room. He had always been so much a part of her life, but as adults they had both stood alone, going their separate ways. Robin into the heart of the music scene, and Melody staying on the fringes, needing quiet and order.

Finally she nodded. She was going to miss Robbie, but she could not cling to him now that Robin was here. 'Two weeks,' she echoed. 'I'll have the songs ready for you next week in LA.'

'You'd better,' he retorted, smiling. 'Are they good?'

'Wait and see.' They both knew she would not share them until the work was finished, even though there was little to do now but the final polishing. 'See you in LA in two weeks,' she whispered, and although he did not leave for two more days that was their real farewell.

She should have been in the music-room that evening, but the soundproofing would block out the telephone if it rang. Wednesday night. Scott.

She was right beside the telephone when it rang, sitting in one of Charlie's big chairs in the living-room.

'How's Robbie?' he asked.

'Fine.' She settled into the deep chair, her legs curled up. 'Robin's putting him to bed right now. The doctor says the hernia looks as if it won't need surgery.'

'And Robin?' He sounded as if he were close, perhaps only a block away.

'Good. He's sad about Donna. And he wants to meet you, to ask about her. He and Robbie are going to LA in a couple of days.' And she was going to miss them terribly. She would be following soon, but she knew that she would not feel this sense of family in the madhouse of the practice sessions for Robin's new album.

'I'll be back on the tenth of June, for two weeks. We'll get together then.'

We? Did he mean to come to her? Or just to see Robin and the baby? She stared at the library of music on the far wall and told herself that this was her life. Stable, her hideaway on the islands. She had no room for what he did to her. Hadn't she come here to find herself, to concentrate on writing songs?

'And the music?' he asked, as if he sensed the motion of her thoughts.

'Almost done.' Next Wednesday she would be in Los Angeles with the tapes. She almost said it, told him what hotel so he could call there. Then she stopped herself, afraid she was taking too much for granted, assuming he wanted to know her movements. In the end she changed her words to, 'What's up in the Arctic?'

'Ice.' His voice was wry. 'Lots of ice. We've spent the whole week fighting it.'

'How do you break ice? Do you just ram into it?'

He explained how the ship rode up on to the ice until the ice knife under the water broke through. Sometimes the knife under the bow wasn't enough. Yesterday *Jonathan Cartier* had jammed in the ice. Scott described how he had got clear by rocking the ship, pumping water from port to starboard tanks inside the ship.

'Actually,' he said, 'I pushed buttons and talked a lot. It was the engineers who did the work. Lots of noise,' he added with a laugh. 'I slammed the throttles from full ahead to full astern so many times, the chief engineer was ready to come up on the bridge and have my head.'

Five minutes. It was over so soon. Then she was alone with her thoughts and a clear image of Scott sitting across from her, as if they had talked for hours.

Why did he call? Once he had called someone named Caroline. Did he call her now, from the frozen north? Melody hugged herself, wishing she knew where this was going. It was one thing to write wild, emotional songs, but she liked to know where her life was heading. Maybe it was all the years of their childhood, of rambling from backstage room to backstage room, but when Charlie and Amanda had parked the twins in Queen Charlotte, Melody had vowed she was going to keep control of her own life after that. She'd slipped, getting caught up in the music scene when her own songs had started to sell, trying to keep up with the madhouse of the recording industry, of Peter with his demands that she fit the image of a popular song-writer and the fiancée of an upwardly mobile talent agent.

Upwardly mobile! God, she hated that phrase. It summarised all her agonies in Los Angeles. No matter how hard she had tried, it had never quite worked. Thank God for Jeff, who had shown her what she was doing with a few critical words.

She shivered, wishing Scott were there to light the fire for her. She was scared. Things were happening. She was losing control, and she knew that she could not hide from the changes. She was not sure what she wanted, but knew that, when Scott Alexander had walked into her home with a baby in his arms, her life had changed. It was never going to be the same again.

CHAPTER SEVEN

MELODY stayed to watch the recording sessions. Robin was surprised, but did not ask her why. Peter was less restrained.

'As your agent, I'm glad to see you're coming to your senses,' he told her as they stood together in the back of the control room. She was wearing jeans and a bulky sweater, and he had already told her that she should dress up more, you never knew when you might run into a news man. Now he said, 'You should be here until the recording's done. Friday I'm booking the Chapels for a party. You'll——'

'No.' She looked at him. He was tall and thin and nervy, his blond hair carefully waved across his forehead, his eyes watchful. 'No, Peter. I'm not doing any publicity stuff. Robin's the performer, not me.'

He was gearing up to argue. He was a good agent, and she knew she would be crazy to leave his agency, but he was not going to dominate her life. She cut off his words quickly. 'Peter, I'll do interviews, even a talk show while I'm here if you really think it's important, but I'm not going on display with rounds of parties and angling for gossip columns.' She shook off his frown and said firmly, 'I hate cocktail parties and I loathe publicity dinners and I won't do it.'

He opened his mouth to protest and she snapped, 'Accept it, Peter.' It was an old argument with them by now, but one she was determined never to lose again. 'Now stop talking and let me hear what's happening with this song.'

She turned away and forgot Peter as she watched Robin and his band turning her poetry into what had to be a hit song when it was released. Even the cynical sound man had a moody look in his eyes as he twirled the dials in the control room. As she listened, she could almost pretend that this was everything, that she would walk from here back to her island retreat and into her music-room where the world could not invade.

She left in the third week of recording, taking a jet from Los Angeles to Vancouver where she retrieved her van from the parking lot. It was time for her to deal with what was happening to her.

She could have telephoned. She had his number, the telephone that would ring at his house on Cortes Island. She had never been to the island, had never seen the little harbour where he had once told her he was building his home. But he would be back there by now. At least, he would have left the Beaufort Sea. She had looked on her map when he called, but even now she didn't know if the Beaufort was part of the Arctic Ocean or not. The map wasn't clear and she had not asked. She should know, she thought absently. He worked up there, and he had her life in turmoil.

She had no idea what she would do if he was not there. Leave a note, she told herself sharply, swinging her car on to the ferry at Campbell River. Lord, her life was one long sequence of ferry boats. Ferry from Vancouver to Vancouver Island. The drive up the island to Campbell River, then another ferry to Quadra Island. Scott had picked a spot that was almost as remote as her Queen Charlotte Islands. To get to Cortes, she had discovered, she had to go island hopping. From Quadra, she took another small ferry to Cortes Island. His island hideaway was definitely out of the rat race!

She had no address, just the telephone number and the knowledge that he had property on Gorge harbour. She should have telephoned from Campbell River, where she could get a hotel room if it turned out he wasn't at home. But what the hell would she say? What if he didn't want her here? What if a woman named Caroline answered? God! For all she knew, he might be married to Caroline. He had never said he was single. That was an assumption she had made. She knew so little about him. Incredible, because she felt as if she had known him forever.

'The Gorge?' The grizzled old man walking along the gravel road frowned at her. She had driven off the second ferry and stopped to ask the way. He was wearing old, patched overalls and a lumberjack's shirt, and he had not shaved in years. He frowned at her and gestured. 'Over there. Where else would it be?'

The Gorge. She knew it when she found it. She stopped the car and looked out over the small, enclosed bay, the rock bluff that gave narrow entry to the sea beyond. She could live here, walking out in the morning along the shore, looking up to the green trees, out over the cool, dark water. Neighbours, but not too close. A place for quiet of the heart, and poetry. Songs.

She shoved the van into gear, frightened by the way her thoughts kept doing that, weaving Scott and his world into her dreams as if he could be nowhere else. She heard the wheels crunch as she pulled back on to the road, and she tried to harden her thoughts.

Scott was not the only person who lived on the Gorge. She passed several driveways that led to little worlds on the water. Too many to go knocking on doors hoping for the right one. She remembered the telephone booth back at the ferry landing and wondered if she should go back, call him after all and hold her breath for the note of welcome—or rejection—in his voice.

She drove along the road, following the curve of the bay.

The name was carved on a beautiful, polished piece of cedar hanging at the end of the drive. Alexander. It wasn't an unusual name, but she turned into the drive and stopped when she could see the peak of the roof.

Cedar shakes, still glowing reddish in the sunlight. A new roof that had not had time to weather into the beautiful grey of the shake roofing that was so common in older houses in the north. She took her foot off the brake and let the van roll a few feet.

The house belonged among the trees, at the side of the ocean. All cedar, the style reminiscent of traditional log cabins, but with a modern crispness of line. A warm house, rambling along the curve of the hillside. She could see the edge of a big veranda where he must sit to look out over the water.

And Scott.

He had not seen her. He was at the far end of the house, standing in a clearing among the trees. He was facing away from her, but she saw him swing the axe up. She had not realised until that moment that she would know him anywhere, from any angle.

She had time to leave, to run. She could reverse and quietly crunch her tyres back out of his driveway. He would never know she had been here. She could go back to Queen Charlotte and——

Some things could not be hidden forever. She felt the nervous excitement of needing to know what would be in his eyes when he saw her; the fear that he would see what was in her heart. Love.

She looked down and saw that her hands were clenching the wheel. She released the steering wheel, but her fingers were trembling. She put the van back in gear and rolled down the short hill, coming to rest right behind the shiny black truck.

She stared at it, remembering Scott in her home, their two vehicles sharing a driveway. He had complained about her drive. His was straighter. Perhaps he did everything more logically, more rationally than she did. Cleaned out his driveways and took precautions against dangers and risks.

Risks.

He swung the axe again. On the block, a piece of wood split cleanly, the two parts dropping neatly to the ground. He bent to pick up a piece of wood from the ground and throw it neatly on to the pile. Then the other piece. Then he turned towards the driveway and she could see nothing in his face, certainly not welcome.

She scrambled out of the van, afraid that he would come to her window and tell her to go back. She told herself that there was no reason for him to send her away. Not when he had called her from the Arctic to talk about nothing much, as if he had wanted only to hear her voice.

He was wearing old jeans and a T-shirt from a hotel in Tuktoyaktuk. She stared at it, concentrating on the weird spelling of the Eskimo word as he came closer. Anything to avoid staring up at his face, his eyes.

'Do they wear T-shirts in Tuktoyaktuk?' she asked nervously. 'I thought it would be all fur parkas up there.'

He stopped walking, just out of her reach. 'Summer sun gets up to Tuk for a bit.' His voice was not smiling, nor his body, all muscles and hardness through the dusty jeans and the shirt.

She looked up and his eyes were hard, too, with none of the welcome she had hoped to see. So the telephone calls had been for Robbie, not for her. She swallowed. 'I wasn't sure if I could find this place. All I knew was

Gorge harbour, on Cortes Island.' She shifted from one foot to the other, the heels of her sandals sinking into soft soil. She looked down and saw she was standing on new grass.

He said, 'I don't imagine you had much trouble. At least I was home.'

'Did you call me again? I was in LA.' Had he? Or had he come, knocking on her locked door? She wished she had not come today, because this was not a man she could open up and talk to. Not the same man who had walked into her house with a baby, who had called and chatted about icebreakers over satellite telephone.

He pushed back a damp lock of sandy brown hair that had been clinging to his forehead. She bit her lip and wondered how to change this from a tense, uneasy staring match into something friendlier. 'It's a warm day for chopping wood, isn't it?'

He shrugged.

She caught herself before she gnawed on her lip. She pushed her hands into the deep pockets of her red cotton skirt and wondered if he thought she looked too garish in red, wondered if he thought she looked nice at all. She had put on fresh lipstick on the ferry, had brushed her hair although it was already smooth waves and healthy shine.

He pushed his hands into the pockets of his jeans, pulling the fabric tight. 'What do you want, Melody?'

Her eyes followed the stretch of the denim, then jerked back to his face. She knew her colour was high. Had he noticed her looking? If so, there was nothing in his face. No smile, no warm teasing light in his hazel eyes.

Where was the sense that she could read his thoughts, that they were talking without words? She looked away to the warm cedar of his home, the water beyond rippled by a late-afternoon breeze.

'Can I come in?' She hated the note of pleading that somehow seeped into her voice.

He shrugged and turned away towards the house.

She struggled over a lump in her throat and managed to make her own voice impatient. 'If you don't want me to be here, I'll go back.' She might as well. She was not going to be able to tell him.

He turned to look at her. 'How are you going to get back? Swim?'

'The ferry.' She had to look away. Lord, this was terrible! She said, 'I think I'd better go. Now.'

He didn't say anything to that at first, but she could not seem to move. Then, finally, he said gently, 'Melody, the last ferry left five minutes ago.' Then he turned and led the way up on to his front veranda.

'Go ahead,' he said, stopping to take his boots off on the veranda. 'Go on inside.'

She would have liked to stay on the veranda for a moment, to look out over his rocky beach and the small harbour, but his impatient voice made her nervous. She followed his gesture and found herself in a big, open room, hardly furnished except for an easy chair and a sofa. And two walls filled with books.

The room did not seem bare. Here, as outside, he had used the warm cedar that grew so plentifully on the coast. The floor was some kind of hardwood, she thought, glowing and beautiful. The fireplace was the most modern thing in the room, styled to look traditional, but with glass doors that allowed light and heat to flow into the room, while controlling the air flow for efficient heating.

'Do you like it?'

She swung around. He was just inside the doorway. He looked more approachable to her without shoes. 'Yes,' she said, not smiling because he wasn't. For a second she thought he was anxious for her answer, but decided it was just that he was not very happy to have her here. She turned away, moving to the picture framed over the fire. 'Ice fields?' she asked. 'Somehow, with the fire and this room, they don't seem all that cold.' He didn't answer and she moved to look at the titles on his shelves. 'I thought you said your house was only half finished.'

'This half,' he answered, moving to the fire. She felt a blast of heat and heard the crackling as he opened the glass doors and bent to feed in more wood. 'The living-room and the kitchen are mostly done, except I've got to go shopping for some furniture one of these days. If you want to see bare walls, framing and joists, there's the back half, and upstairs.'

'Oh.' She would have been happy to have a tour, but he had not spoken as if it were really an invitation.

He stood up and she jerked back to the books. It was not getting better. She wished painfully that she had not come. She watched as he pushed his hair back, releasing a small chip of wood that had been caught in the waves.

'Look, can you fend for yourself here while I get cleaned up?'

'Yes.' She made an abrupt gesture. 'Of course I can. Go ahead.'

He frowned and seemed about to say something, then nodded and walked out of the room towards the back of the house. The unfinished part, he had said, but she heard the sound of water running a moment later. A shower, she thought, so more than the kitchen must be finished.

She would have put on music, but there was no stereo. She went to the books instead, but they were almost as intimidating as the granite of his eyes. She took out a geology book and tried to absorb the words when she opened it, then gave up and pulled out a book of tall ships. She stood, turning pages, listening to the water running somewhere close by. Scott's shower. She turned another page and admired an old boat with an abundance of white, square sails.

When the telephone rang, she almost dropped the book. Then a door opened or closed somewhere and Scott's voice called to her.

'Get that, will you? Take a message.'

She answered the telephone. It was a woman calling, her voice sharp and startled. 'I must have the wrong number.' The voice rattled off a number.

'No, you've dialled right,' said Melody, looking down at the number on Scott's phone.

'Where's Scott?'

'He's . . . busy. Can I take a message?'

'No, I—— Yes, all right.' The voice became brisk. 'Ask him to bring my nightgown and my toilet things in to Campbell River. The nightgown's in the drawer in his dresser, and—— He'll know where to find it.'

The line went dead. Melody put down the receiver. Well, that was plain enough. She pushed her hands into her pockets and tried to tell herself that she was curious about this room, about the scenery. Anything but the woman.

When Scott came into the room, she was at the window, looking out at the trees. She did not turn when she spoke. That way she was able to keep her voice casual.

'The bedroom must be done, too.' She heard the bite in her own voice, but could not seem to stop it. 'Because she said she left her nightgown in your dresser, and would you bring it to her. And her toilet bag.' She turned and Scott was in the doorway. She added, 'She didn't say what her name was.'

'Caroline.' His hair was still damp, just starting to wave as it dried. He was wearing a pair of corduroy trousers and a soft, bulky sweater and his face was flushed uncomfortably. He said, 'She——'

Melody made a sharp gesture. 'Don't tell me!' She had to be crazy, letting herself dream about him. 'I knew there was a Caroline. You called her from Queen Charlotte. I just thought—I don't know what I thought.' She gulped and said, 'That she didn't matter, I guess.'

'Yeah,' he said uncomfortably. 'Look, I——'

She spun away from him, but where was there to go? 'You don't have to explain anything. It's not—you don't owe me any explanations, or——'

He laughed harshly. 'You mean I can sleep with anyone I like, and you don't give a damn?'

She smoothed her hands on her skirt. 'No,' she whispered. 'I—I don't mean that. I—I just don't want to hear about her.'

'Hell!' She jumped and he said, 'Damn it, Melody! I'm sorry, but—I don't—— If there are rules for this sort of thing, I don't know them. Caroline—we were friends.' He grimaced and said, 'Not all my friends leave their nightgowns in my drawers.'

Were, he had said. Past tense. She bit her lip. 'She's not a friend any more?'

'Not that kind,' he said. 'Not since—— It was you I called when I was up in the Beaufort, not Caroline. It was you I went to see the minute I——'

And she had not been home. Her fingers curled into her skirt and she whispered, 'I was going to tell you. The last time you phoned me. I—I almost gave you the number of the hotel in LA, where I would be. But I—I don't know. I guess I wasn't sure why you were calling me, if you would call again.'

She could feel the flush in her cheeks, but the ice was gone from his eyes. She could see the long breath that escaped his body, leaving it relaxed. He smiled and asked, 'Do we owe each other any more explanations?'

She shook her head, because she was not ready to tell him her secrets yet. He said, 'All right, then. Why don't you stop looking as if you want to run? I won't bite.'

'Won't you?'

He must have seen the nervousness in her smile, because he said, 'Melody, you may be stranded here until the morning ferry, but I won't expect you to share my bed, if that's what you're worried about.'

'Oh.' She felt deflated, confused.

'Shall we find something to eat?' he suggested. 'Have you had supper?' She shook her head and he said, 'Stop looking as if I'm the big bad wolf and we'll get some supper.'

She followed him through an unfinished hallway into a big kitchen. She was surprised at the modern brightness after the warm, glowing darkness of the living-room.

'No, Caroline did not design it,' he said sharply, reading her thoughts. 'I did. With the help of the cabinet-maker I hired.'

'I like it,' she said, and half smiled when she realised that her voice was placating. Then he laughed and somehow everything was all right.

'Omelettes?' he suggested.

'All right.'

She chopped the onions and he wiped her eyes when she cried from the fumes. Then he burned the omelette and insisted that he could do better.

It was going to be all right. She told herself that, watching him burn the omelette. 'Charlie always insisted he could cook,' she said, laughing, wrinkling her nose. 'You really burnt it, didn't you?'

'Yeah.' He opened a cupboard door and exposed a flip-top rubbish bin. 'Let's start from scratch. And this time I'll watch the stove instead of watching you.'

She gasped and he said, 'And who's Charlie?'

'My father. And he can't cook. When he threatens to, it means he's hungry and Amanda—my mother—better get in the kitchen or else he'll smoke up the whole house.' She smiled fondly. 'He's a real manipulator.'

'You love them?' He was keeping his eye on the pan this time, and the omelette came out of the pan light and aromatic.

'Yes. It wasn't a very conventional childhood, and their footloose lifestyle doesn't suit me, but Robin and I always knew they loved us.' He nodded and she remembered that his background had been foster-homes and probably not enough love.

'What about men?' he asked, and she did not turn the subject back to childhood. Sometime, he might want to share his with her. Maybe.

'Only one,' she said. 'We were engaged. That was when I thought being a song-writer meant I had to live in the madhouse with the musicians. He thought so, too.' She shrugged. 'He wanted me to be someone else.'

He was watching her. Somehow, she did not mind. He asked, 'And what did you want?'

She met his eyes. 'Not Peter.'

'Peter?' he repeated. 'Jeff called and asked you to call him back. At Peter's.'

She nodded. 'He's my talent agent. And Robin's. And Jeff's, for that matter. He's good, but I'm not in love with him. Sometimes I wonder if I ever was.'

He managed not to burn the second omelette. They sat together in the breakfast nook, eating slowly. 'It's good,' she said.

'What about Jeff?'

She looked at him. He was watching her, perhaps looking for a reaction. She wondered if she should resent the questions, but she wanted him to care. 'He's a good friend. When I was going nuts trying to be the fastest rat on the treadmill, he helped me see what I was doing to myself.' She stirred the omelette and said slowly, 'I've only been writing my songs in Queen Charlotte for a couple of years. Before that—— Jeff helped me find the equipment I needed, and he came visiting and brought me gossip and—— He's been with Robin's band from the beginning.' He was waiting for her to say something else and she said, 'We've never been lovers. He's more like another brother.'

'Caroline and I were lovers. You know that.' He stirred the omelette around on his plate without eating any. 'I think she appealed to me because she's all tied up in her career and didn't need me.' He shrugged. 'Maybe I appealed to her because I wasn't asking her to give up her independence or make any commitments that would interfere with her plans to become head of her department at the college.'

She frowned. It sounded cold-blooded.

He said, 'My parents died when I was eight years old. I started learning then that it's best not to tie your happiness to someone else's whim.' He said it flatly, as if it were a fact that had not changed.

'What about Donna?' He did not answer, but his sister was gone. Another lesson that might make it hard to trust in someone else. She dropped her fork on to the plate, and whispered, 'What about Robbie?' But in her heart, she was wondering, What about me?

He washed up their few dishes. She dried, opening cupboards to find the places for the plates and glasses.

'I thought of getting a dishwasher,' he told her as he rinsed out the sink.

'You could put it over there, couldn't you? There's room at the end of the counter. Actually, I don't use the dishwasher in my house all that much. Just when company descends.'

'Does that happen often?' He grinned.

'Men knocking on my door, handing me babies? All the time.' She fell abruptly silent then, thinking of what she had come to tell him, but she wanted very much to enjoy this evening first. 'Sometimes it's a madhouse. Charlie and Amanda send friends sometimes. Can we go for a walk? Would you show me the rest of your house?'

'Outside first,' he said. 'While there's still light.'

He loaned her a big, bulky sweater that hung halfway down her thighs, then he took her out walking along his rocky beach. He told her about the old man who lived around the curve of the bay, who remembered when the Gorge was wild territory accessible only by private boat. They speculated together on whether the pirates had ever discovered what a perfect pirates' den Gorge harbour would make, and he told her about his plans to have a wharf put in.

'I've got to straighten out the water rights first,' he said, and she memorised the lines that formed on his forehead as he concentrated on the prospect of getting through red tape.

'Would you have a boat?' She had never been out in the water in anything but a ferry.

'I don't think so, at least not a big one.' He stopped, looking back at his property, his house, as the setting sun bathed it in warm tones. 'I've got friends who have a sail-boat. It would be nice to have a place for them to tie up when they come cruising up here. I've got a runabout on the trailer in the garage. It's enough for what

I want, good for a run into Campbell River in an emergency or an afternoon salmon fishing.'

Later, she could not have said what else they talked about. Everything. Nothing. It was dark when he brought her back into his house. They went first to her van for her suitcase, which he insisted on carrying for her.

He did not kiss her. The moon was rising as the sun went down, but when he put her case into his bedroom, he said neutrally, 'You're tired. Get some sleep. The morning is soon enough for a tour of the house.'

Then he left her alone in the bedroom and she was crazy enough to open the drawers until she found one drawer which was empty except for a lacy black nightgown.

Melody had never looked good in black. She caught herself before she slammed the drawer shut, knowing that Caroline made no real difference. Caroline was history in Scott's life now. But what was Melody?

CHAPTER EIGHT

THE upstairs was a mess, sawdust and plaster dust everywhere. Scott told Melody to be careful not to trip over anything, and that it was going to be two more bedrooms with dormer windows and views of the ocean.

'And this part?' she asked, standing in the middle of the biggest, empty room.

He shrugged and saw her eyes crinkle with laughter. 'I don't know. I'll finish it, I guess, and wait for all my friends to descend on me, looking for a place to sleep.'

Looking at Melody as she stood at the newly framed window, he almost told her it would make a terrific music-room. That window could be shuttered easily. The walls could have soundproofing added. He had not yet put the plaster on them.

It scared him, thinking like that. He did not want to be aware of every move Melody made, every breath she took, but when she breathed he felt the pressure on his lungs. He liked the way she always went to the windows when she entered a room, as if the view meant as much to her as the walls. Caroline had walked around frowning at the exposed joists, the unfinished floors. Melody seemed to see through the construction to the dream he had of his finished home.

He did not want to compare her to Caroline. Because there was no comparison, and that frightened him most of all. Calling home from the Beaufort had suddenly come to mean talking to Melody.

He remembered the third time he had gone to the rig to call her, listening to the empty ringing. He had felt a sick fear that he would never talk to her again, never hold her in his arms again. He had waited for the next week, the next chance to call. Had waited for some message. Had finally flown out of Tuk to Calgary and gone to her island instead of to his own.

Her van had been gone. Her house had been dark. Empty houses and closed doors. He had managed to guess that she had gone to the recording sessions in Los Angeles. She had not said she was going, but he knew that was the deadline she had been working against in her song-writing.

It was not that she was gone, but that she had not bothered to tell him. As if it were not important enough. As if *he* were not important enough. That was when he realised that he had done exactly what he had vowed never to do.

An affair, he had told himself. After all, Melody was committed to her song-writing. She liked being a recluse between visits from friends and her brother. She was not looking for a deep relationship, for commitments or risks. Neither was he, damn it!

He had not expected to find that he was the one with his heart out. The discovery, standing on her dark doorstep, had sent him back here, panicked and determined to throw himself into construction, into reading about geology. Anything but thinking about her.

He had ploughed into the books. Every year he tried to learn something to fill the gaps in his education. He had never gone back to school, but he tried to make up for it by reading, studying, learning about the world he lived in. This year, he had decided, he would pursue books with a vengeance and to hell with the notion of getting a stereo to learn more about music so that he could share it with Melody.

As a child he had vowed never to give anyone the power to hurt him again by walking out on him or kicking him out. So why was he up here, showing her his home and hoping she would like it? Why was he fighting the impulse to tell her how he could change it for her to share?

An affair, for God's sake. A friendship. Not a life.

'What's wrong?' she asked, turning to him as if she could see the turmoil inside him. She was wearing his sweater again, because the heating was not installed upstairs yet.

He pushed his hair back. 'Nothing. I've got to work on the fence at the back today. I want to put stain on before it rains.'

It would be better after she was gone. Then he would make himself remember that she was Robbie's aunt, too dangerous for touching.

'Oh?' She made it a question, asking, 'Do you want me to go?' She bit her lip.

He shoved his hands into his pockets to avoid touching her. 'You're likely to get paint-spattered if you don't.' He tried not to think about making love to her with the firelight playing on her glowing, naked flesh, with her eyes dark and passionate as he bent to kiss and possess.

'How's Robbie?' he asked desperately, pushing away his over-active imagination. She had been here since yesterday afternoon, yet somehow there had been no time to talk about his nephew.

He listened to her talking about Robbie, about her brother, and he knew it wasn't going to work. He was going to touch her, and if she did not run or scream, he was in trouble.

'You could stay a while,' he said, harshly cutting across her account of Robin's running into a reporter when he was out walking the baby in his new pram.

She fell silent, staring at him, her eyes wide and black and unfathomed. What the hell was he doing? Setting himself up to be slapped in the face? So she had made love with him. Once. It didn't mean—no, damn it! He didn't *want* it to mean more! He made certain nothing showed in his voice. He said, 'If you're taking a holiday, you could do some painting, some hammering if you like. You need a holiday.' She half smiled and he grinned, although inside he was afraid she would say yes and he knew he was in too deep. 'Or just sit around and read,' he added, and heard the hopefulness in his own voice.

Her hands moved to push into her pockets, but the sweater was in her way. He let his own hands free and possessed hers. Her fingers were cold, trembling. He rubbed them between his hands, to warm them.

She said, 'I'd better take the painting. You don't have a lot of light reading in those shelves.'

'We can go into Campbell River and raid the book stores,' he offered. Then he released her hands because he could feel the tension growing inside himself. He tried to tell himself it was nothing more than a shared holiday, an affair that would be a pleasant memory next year, but he kept remembering how he had felt standing on her doorstep, knowing she was gone and not knowing where.

Melody linked her hands together when he released them. In a second he would kiss her. She could see his eyes turning from hazel to a low fire, his firm lips parting just slightly. She knew that she had to stop him.

'No?' he said, and it was only half a question. He was picking up something from the tension in her, or did he simply read the thoughts right out of her mind? He stepped back and she saw relief in his eyes, as if he had not really wanted to want her.

'Not——' Not right now. Not yet. She licked her lips and knew the words were not going to come. Practising saying it was one thing, but this was impossible. She wanted to stay, take the holiday he had offered. She wanted to put on an old shirt of Scott's and stand beside him, painting stain on to his fence. She wanted to read his books, to watch him lighting the fire in the fireplace. She wanted to talk and listen and share the silences . . . to make love with him again.

She knew she could not possibly stay without telling him first. She gulped and said, 'I guess I'd better go.'

'Why did you come?'

She could not read anything in his face. He was waiting, watching, the ship's commander suspending judgement. Crazily, that made it easier, because she could harden her own voice too, and her mind. She turned away from him so that he could not see into her eyes. She stared through the window at the smooth, shining water of the little bay, the narrow gorge that opened out to the ocean. She said, 'I thought you should know, that you had a right to know . . . I'm pregnant.'

She turned and he was staring at her. She wasn't sure what it was in his eyes. He blinked and she thought maybe it was shock. Of course it would be shock. She had wanted it to be joy, but she should have known to keep the fairy-tales in her music-room.

He said slowly, 'Say that again.'

She didn't. He had heard her the first time. She could not keep staring at him, wondering what on earth he was reading in her eyes. Was he reading her young dreams of happy-ever-afters? Dreams that had been twisting their way into her mind ever since that morning when he had turned up on her front doorstep.

He pushed a rough hand through his hair, frowned and asked, 'But how——'

'I wasn't on the Pill or anything.'

It was anger now, in his eyes, although his voice was as cold as the ocean where he piloted his ships. 'I asked you and you said——'

She remembered the warm fire, the heat that had flashed between them, undeniable as if they were two halves of one soul aching for unity. She gulped and admitted, 'You asked if I was prepared, and I—I didn't mean birth control. I just——'

He turned away from her. She did not realise he was going downstairs until she heard his boots on the stairs, steady and deliberate. She followed him, her sandals clattering down the stairs. She came to a stop in the living-room, out of breath, staring at him across the room. He was standing at the door and she wondered if he was intending to walk out on her, or to kick her out.

'Scott——'

He said flatly, 'I don't believe it. You can't be that naïve!'

Couldn't she? She had turned thirty last Christmas Day, but she had never really loved before, not in the way a woman loved a man. All her loving had been in songs, in fantasy. Perhaps she had hidden in her own fantasies, finding them safer than what she felt now.

She had been insane to come. She had thought——

He had a right to know, that's what she had thought. But under that, some crazy part of her had thought that he might feel what she did: a wild warm excitement, a rightness that the touch of a loving stranger had given birth to a life. Fate. Belonging.

She did not want to love anyone like this, so painfully. Not unless he could love her back. She pushed her hands into her pockets. She was cold in spite of the fire he had lit in his fireplace, despite the warm cedar. It was his eyes, and she knew there was never going to be anything for them.

Except the child they had created.

He was tensed up like a wire, his eyes almost glazed, his jaw clenched. Even his hands were clenched into fists at his side. What did he think she was going to do to him? Did he think she was trying to trap him into marriage?

She jerked her eyes away from him, but he was all around. The picture, the books, the fire, even the glimpses of water outside. She said raggedly, 'Look, I'm not interested in being lectured. I only came to tell you because——' she gulped '—because it's not the sort of thing you put in a letter. And I thought you had a right to know.'

She had thought he would welcome her, welcome her child. Secret fantasy, not acknowledged even to herself. Crazy woman. Fantasising song-writer. Poet.

He said flatly, 'What do you expect of me?'

He was staring at her and she could feel her eyes burning, her lids open too wide and her skin stretched too tightly over her face. If she didn't get out of here, she was going to cry. She must not let him see her cry, not when he was looking at her like that, his eyes harsh and his mouth a line of judgement.

She saw him swallow. His nostrils were flared, his voice bitterly angry. 'What did you expect, Melody? Did you think I would welcome your news? What was I supposed to say? Let's get married and have a happy-ever-after?'

She shook her head, although maybe that *was* what she had dreamed. He prowled angrily across his living-room and came back to confront her.

'What the devil do I know about families? About babies? Nothing!' His face was all harsh lines and angles. 'I can barely remember my own mother. All I know is from the outside, looking in. I haven't a damn clue in hell how to be on the inside, and you'd be crazy to think we could—we could...'

'Love each other?' It hurt to swallow, hurt more to whisper, 'Couldn't we try?'

'If that's what you thought——' He cleared his throat, turned to stare grimly at a tree outside. 'Why do you think I brought Robbie to you in the first place? I was desperate to get him off my hands. A baby needs a father who knows what the hell he's doing. All I know about families is what I learned as a kid. I learned how not to get thrown out. If I did enough chores, I got to stay. Maybe.'

Her hands reached out towards him, wanting to soothe the pain she could feel in him. 'Scott——'

He jerked away. 'A woman needs a man who can love both her and her baby without messing it up.' He started prowling again, came to rest in front of her, staring at her bleakly.

She said, 'You're afraid to try, afraid to take a chance. We could——'

'No, we *couldn't*!' He crammed his hands deeply into his pockets and turned to glare at the fire.

She stared at a place in the middle of the window and said tightly, 'The baby's not going to go away, Scott.'

His hands curled into fists inside his pockets. 'I'll—we'll make some kind of—some sort of financial arrangement.'

Oh, God! She could feel the tears coming. This was worse than she could have imagined. She walked past him. Then she was on the veranda, staring at nothing, and he was behind her. She made herself move, across the open expanse to the stairs, down to the grass.

She got to her van and the keys were still there. She had not even thought of keys, of her bag. She stared at the dashboard and knew she could not walk back into that house for her bag. It was in his bedroom, with her suitcase.

She turned the starter, but nothing happened except for the whine of the buzzer telling her to do up her seatbelt. She sat there, staring at the windscreen, and finally she realised that she had forgotten to put the car in parking gear when she stopped. The emergency brake was on, but the gear-shift was in gear.

If she sat here long enough, messing up the simple job of driving away, he would come through the door and she would have to look at his eyes again and know he was never going to care for her in the way she needed.

Never going to love her.

She must not cry. Whatever she did, she had to keep from letting the tears out until she was somewhere far away. The engine caught, finally, and she started reversing.

He was there, standing in the doorway, the back door, staring after her, blurry through the moisture in her eyes. She kept going, trying to go straight back and steady. He did nothing to stop her.

A giggle escaped her, but it was half a sob. What was he going to do about her suitcase? Would he send it to her? She might open her door to a knock and find a courier there, her suitcase returned. If this went on, his bedroom would be littered with mementoes of women who had once shared his touch but not his heart.

She was out of his driveway before she realised that she could not go on. She would willingly have risked driving forever without her driver's licence, just to avoid facing him again. But she could not even get off his island without her bag. No money for ferry fares, no credit cards for petrol. Not even a bank card to get cash from some strange, shiny bank.

*　*　*

There was no choice. She could sit here on a rock, looking out over the water forever, but the fact was that she could not get off Cortes Island without at least her purse, her money.

She had to go back and get it.

She hugged herself, realising that she still wore his sweater. She should have taken it off, put on her own jacket which was secure inside her suitcase. In his bedroom. It was one thing to say it, in her mind. I'll go back. Different to drive up and face him again. She could feel the nervousness quivering in her stomach, the adrenalin pumping, telling her to run, get the hell away from this whole mess. Hide somewhere. Plug herself in to some music and make the world go away.

She wrapped her arms tighter around herself. Around his baby. She wanted to think of it as hers, but she wanted it to be a boy with sandy brown hair that waved just a little. And hazel eyes that would look at her and smile. Oh, lord! This was terrible. She was turning into a stupid ball of jelly, tears coming every time she thought of his name, his eyes, his smile. Even his cold frown.

She would have nightmares of saying, 'I'm having your baby. When you touched my soul, we made a life of love.' Nightmares of her lips open and her eyes vulnerable, and his hard rejection, in his eyes and his jaw and the broad, hard back he turned on her.

He did not want her, did not want her child. She had read fantasies into the way he had held Robbie tenderly, the way he had moved into her life and her heart with crazy little actions like tending her fire and doing her dishes and cooking her breakfast.

Something moved out on the water. An otter? Or perhaps a dolphin? She was too far away, too high up to see clearly. She rubbed her eyes and it disappeared as the water came clear. She could not stay here forever.

The day would go, and she would be stuck here for another night. She had to get away, back to her own place where she could close doors against the world.

Cars kept driving by on the road behind her. She had pulled the van into a clearing, had walked to the rock on the water's edge. This didn't seem to be anyone's property, just a clearing on the Gorge. But sometimes the cars slowed and eventually someone might stop and try to talk to her.

Hi. Stranger around here?

Are you lost?

Or it might be Scott, come with her bag, helping her to be gone from his life.

She could not hide out on this rock forever. Could not face him either. Maybe on another day, after she got her defences up. She tried to turn what she was feeling into a song, but the aching would not turn into fantasy. Maybe it never would, and she would always feel it as a wound she could not erase with music.

Damn! Action. She needed action. She had always hated movies where the heroine agonised all over the screen, huddling in misery instead of getting up and doing something.

If he was outside, painting as he had said, then perhaps she could sneak into his house and get her purse out. He might never even know she had been there. Then she could get off his bloody island and back to her own.

She was not sure how far she had driven along the bay, knew only that she could see what she thought was the peak of his roof. If she drove back, he would see her van when it entered his drive. On the other hand, she could not safely park on the road by his drive. She might break into his house for her bag, then come back to find another driver had sideswiped her van because she'd parked on a blind curve. That was all she would need to turn this day into even more of a disaster!

She decided to walk back, but first she pulled the van further from the road, so that it was half hidden by an old maple tree. When she walked to the road and looked back, the brown van hardly showed from the road. Just in case Scott had driven after her, it was best if the van did not show.

Why fool herself? He was not going to come after her. She had walked away, had saved him the bother of sending her off. But why had he talked as if he cared last night, asking about the men in her life? And this morning, hadn't it been he who'd suggested she stick around?

But that was before she had told him about the baby. He might have been willing to love her a little, for a while, but there wasn't enough love in him for both her and a baby.

It was in the whole pattern of his life. There was no one in the centre of his life. He wanted it that way. She should have listened more closely, because last night, as they'd talked during his second try at cooking omelettes, he had told her that commitment wasn't in his dictionary. Until this morning, she hadn't realised that he meant he was afraid of trying.

It was a longer walk than she had thought, especially in the flimsy sandals that had been good for driving, good for standing around the studio in LA. Not good for walking the gravel shoulder of the road, but with the occasional car coming past fast and unexpectedly she dared not walk on the road itself.

There was a time, as a child, when her feet had been tough from the beaches of the Queen Charlotte islands. Then she would have thrown off her sandals and gone barefoot on the gravel, but now she gritted her teeth and tried to pretend she was not developing a blister where the strap rubbed across her big toe.

A car came from behind, slowing to a crawl. She kept moving, staring at the trees, hoping the driver would not stop. She did not want to talk to anyone, simply could not handle even the most basic social contact at this moment. After a moment of hesitation, the driver surged past and she was alone again.

How many more properties until she came to the board with his name on it? The next corner, perhaps. She looked down and plodded on. Then she put her foot down on a small rock and her ankle turned, jarring her whole body and leaving her with a sick feeling in her stomach. She closed her eyes and let the pain flow through her, and after a while it faded. She flexed the ankle and decided it was all right, and after a while the ache faded as she walked on.

His driveway. Where was Scott? She moved slowly, walking on the mossy growth at the side of the trees, hoping for silence and invisibility, wishing there were some other way to get off Cortes Island. Crawling back into the lion's den wasn't her first choice, but the only alternative was breaking into some stranger's home and stealing another person's purse.

Oh, lord! She should have used her fantasy time to weave stories of burglars slipping invisibly into log houses.

She heard him before she saw him. He was at the far end of the house. She could hear the slam of his axe hitting a block of wood, the thud of the splintered piece falling to the ground. Steady, regular, his axe smashing violently into the firewood. Taking out his anger, she decided. There was a violence to the rhythm that had not been there the day before.

She did not have to wonder why he was not painting, his chosen task for the day. Chopping wood was more satisfactory. He was probably fantasising that it was her head on the block as he swung. She shook that thought away. Foolish. She was the one with the fantasies. He kept his life under control, each event planned. His house was growing as he had planned. His nephew was firmly in his natural father's hands, as Scott had planned.

Her pregnancy had not been planned, because she had told him she was prepared and he had believed her. So he was rejecting it in a storm of wood-chips. Did that mean that he felt something other than simple rejection? If so, by the time he had finished piling the fresh wood, he would have worked out a plan to get even this event under control.

Some kind of financial arrangement, he had said. She did not want to be part of some cold plan for organising unwanted... unwanted lovers... unwanted babies.

She crossed the driveway to the far side, slipping into the trees. Thank goodness she had not put on the red skirt today, but a leaf-green one with a white blouse. And Scott's sweater covered the brilliance of her blouse pretty well. She thought that she might blend into the trees if he looked up.

He was wearing a checked shirt, so he had changed since she left. Maybe that was what had sent him out here in a fury of chopping: finding her bag and suitcase in his bedroom. She took a deep breath and stepped on a stick that snapped loudly.

She froze. From the water she could hear a faint whisper of water on rock. From the woodpile, nothing. She could not see him, either, but then the red checked shirt emerged as he stood up. Breathless, she waited for him to turn and seek her out of the trees with sharp eyes.

A bird cried overhead. Abruptly, Scott moved, then she saw the glint of the axe just before she heard the impact of metal on wood. He had not heard her, or had decided that the sound was nothing but the natural sounds of the forest.

She could not get her lungs working properly again until she had the bulk of his house between them. Then she stopped and sank to the ground, sitting on soft moss and breathing deep, ragged breaths until her heart stopped slamming into her ribs.

It was a good thing she had not set out on a life of crime. It was one thing to contemplate slipping into a house undetected, but the fact was that she was a bloody coward. The thought of Scott coming upon her, standing there with his shoulders squared and demanding harshly what the hell she thought she was doing——

The front door, through the veranda. That way she would not come in view of the woodpile again until she was slipping away. She took her sandals off at the bottom of his steps, remembering how they had clattered as she came downstairs only an hour ago. Or was it a lifetime ago?

She pushed the sandals into her big pockets, her fingers curling around the van keys in her right pocket, seeking reassurance that she hadn't lost her keys now, too. Then she went silently up the stairs and on to his veranda.

He had left the front door hanging open, the cool morning flowing into his home. She slipped inside, leaving it open, too. The fire was lower now, just glowing through the glass of the fireplace. He had not put any more wood on. She moved away from its beckoning warmth, away from the living-room, from his books and the picture of the Arctic ice. Into the hallway that was not panelled yet, with bare studs in the wall and the white of electrical wiring running along the studs.

His bedroom door was closed. She knew that she had
left it open, but he would have slammed it closed after
he changed his shirt. Trying to shut her away, because
she had left her possessions behind. She opened it slowly,
quietly. There were no creaking boards or doors in this
house. No mistakes, because he was building it as it
should be. She was the mistake, and she supposed he
was out there regretting that he had ever looked at
Melody Connacher, had ever touched her, had ever loved
her. Because, damn it, he had loved her, whether he admitted it or not. It hadn't been just sex between them.

She thought of Robin's Donna, afraid to trust the man
she loved, to share his life. Twins, she and Robin, living
parallel lives. She shuddered, realising that if there had
been a chance of a relationship with Scott she had blown
it by dumping too much on him, too soon. Babies.
Commitment. Forever. Love. It had felt like love, but
he would not let love in. He had built walls to keep the
loving out.

Her bag was on the dresser. She picked it up and
pushed the strap up over her shoulder. Her suitcase was
sitting open on the floor near the window. She wondered
if she could close it and take it with her, and still be quiet
enough.

Her heart was beating in rhythm with the swing of his
axe. Here, inside, the sound was muffled, but impacting
on her heart. She crossed to the case and pushed her
things down, closed the lid and leaned on it to snap the
locks. Then she froze.

The telephone was ringing. Her eyes flew to the
bedroom door. He had closed it, but it was open now.
If he came into the house to answer the telephone, he
might realise she was here. As she heard the third ring,
the axe bit into the wood again. Perhaps he could not
hear it, or simply did not want to answer.

Was it Caroline? Would he go back to Caroline now? Had Melody read him entirely wrong? He had spoken as if she were the reason that Caroline was history, but that might have been her own desires interpreting his words.

A fourth ring. Five. Then six. If it was Caroline, then she was persistent, and she might win. Melody swallowed a lump and wondered if there was anything she could change by staying, by walking out there to the woodpile and telling him she was in love with him.

It stopped on the ninth ring. There was silence then, not even the sound of the axe biting into wood. The walls of the bedroom seemed to move in and out with each breath she took, the silence echoing and pounding in her ears. Then she heard the door.

Footsteps, not quiet or careful. He was in the kitchen, she thought. She heard the refrigerator open with a sucking sound, then close. A cupboard door. She had not upset the fabric of his life enough to affect his appetite.

She realised then that the room was starting to spin. She sat down on the edge of the bed, afraid she would fall and make a thud that would bring him in here. How long would it be before he went out again? Or might he come to his bedroom and pack her things to get them out of his sight?

She did not hear the door slam. Maybe he left it open again. Or perhaps he did close it, but she was caught in the memory of last night, sleeping in his bed, catching the scent of Scott on the sheets, falling asleep and dreaming that he held her in his arms, that he whispered how much he loved her, how she was the one woman who could turn his life to warmth and closeness.

The first she knew of his leaving the house was the sight of his red checked shirt through the window. She jumped and almost called out. She could not see his face. Only his back, walking away. She got up and went to the window, and there he was, walking towards the back corner of the house with a can of wood stain in his left hand.

Back to normal. He had planned to stain the cedar fence today. At least she had not prevented that.

She left the way she had come, carrying her suitcase and moving in stockinged feet, stopping to put on her sandals when she was on the grass. Out of his house. Out of his life.

CHAPTER NINE

PERCUSSION instruments drowned out the tempo of the bass guitar. Then nothing, just the echo of rhythm in the silence of the room.

Melody dropped her hands from the synthesiser. The multi-track recorder turned silently, recording nothing. She stared at the equipment, knowing it was useless. She had no idea if the song was good or bad. It felt dead, the words without meaning, the notes disconnected. She did not know if the lack was in her, or in the music she had written.

Last night she had reached for the telephone to call Robin, intending to play the music over the telephone and ask him if it was any good. He would have been astounded. She had never let anyone else listen to a song unless she was sure it was good. If she had no confidence in it, she was not willing to share any of her work.

She turned everything off and took the tape out of the recorder, placing it in its protective plastic case. Then she closed the door on the music-room and went out, locking the house.

She went to the radio station, although it was hours too early for *Island Time*. She wanted busy work, so she buried herself in the record library. She picked out other people's music, talked her way through *Island Time*, and felt a little better.

It was returning home that was difficult. It had never bothered her before when the house was empty. If she wanted to talk to the world, there was the ham radio.

And there was the music-room, always before filled with life and feeling. But now, three days living alone and she was ready to climb the walls.

She accepted Bev's invitation to dinner, spent an evening playing with Bev and John's two-year-old holy terror. The next day she went down to the college and picked up a copy of the new calendar; but none of the night-school courses would be starting until September, so that did her no good. She needed something to fill her hours now, to stop her from thinking.

Then she went back to the radio station, into Laurie's office, to ask the station manager about going to work full time.

Laurie was sorting through the results of a survey of listeners, turning endless pages of computer printout. She looked up at Melody, frowning, her lively dark eyes worried.

'Are you sure you want to, Melody? Full time, I wouldn't be able to release you for the recording sessions, you know.'

Melody wondered if she would ever be able to write another song. She could not say that to Laurie.

'Think about it,' said Laurie. 'And if you ever want to talk, I'm here, you know. About anything.'

Friends. She had more friends than she deserved. Jeff and Laurie and John and Bev. Yet she knew that she could not go to any of them for help. She had to be strong, to start planning for herself and the child. She had to find her own answer, not someone else's.

She went to her doctor and came home with a vitamin supplement and a book on looking after herself and the child inside. Queen Charlotte being the small town that it was, she suspected that within twenty-four hours everyone would know Melody Connacher was expecting a child. No one would be likely to say anything, not to her, but there were few secrets in a town this size. She did not think any of her friends would criticise her, but they would expect her eventually to confide in them.

Plans, she thought, and she went down to the basement to start cleaning out the storeroom. It had been waiting ten years or so to be organised, but now seemed a good time. Some of it was bits and pieces of Charlie and Amanda's theatre life. Some of it was from Robin and Melody's youth. She thought that if she cleaned the house, she might find her thoughts tidier, more purposeful.

At least there were the royalties coming in, and with Robin turning so many of her songs into hits Melody and the baby should not have to worry about how to pay the grocery bill for a while. Better if she could write more good songs, but if not she would go back and tell Laurie that she wanted to dedicate all her time to the radio station. She would tell her about the baby, and Laurie would understand.

Crouched on the floor amid the dusty memories, Melody picked up a bundle of paper with a garter holding them together. She slipped the garter off. A blue garter. Something blue for Amanda's wedding?

Love-letters, from Charlie to a younger Amanda. She thought of the letters Robin had written to Donna. Love-letters. Lovers.

She put Charlie's letters back where she had found them, without reading them. They were private, not hers to intrude on. She sat cross-legged on the basement floor, thinking about her parents as lovers for the first time. With a child's narrow view, she had never thought of their romance. She knew them as characters, as friends to each other and their children, as partners on the stage...but not as lovers.

What would they think when she told them she was going to have a child? They would accept it, but they would worry about her. From a distance, she thought wryly, because she and Robin had never been encouraged to lean on their parents. Perhaps that was the pattern they had learned, standing alone, because, despite the ways in which they were close, Robin had not told her of his love for Donna, and Melody was not reaching to tell her twin that she loved a man who did not want loving.

When the knock came, she knew that it would be Scott.

He had been in her mind, lying in the background through everything else, the doctor and the radio station and Charlie's love-letters to Amanda. In a few days, he would be back on his icebreaker in the Beaufort Sea. She had been counting the days. She thought she knew him well enough to know that he would want to settle his loose ends before he left.

She went up the stairs, dusting her hands off on the seat of her jeans. She felt that she was watching herself move, observing herself as she opened the door. Then he was there, in front of her, broad shoulders blocking out the light. His hazel eyes were serious, thoughtful. She wondered what he intended for them, for their child. Her eyes went past him, to the shiny black truck. She thought of the first time she had seen him, Robbie hidden in the truck.

He must have read her thought because he said, 'Nothing in the truck this time. Can I come in?'

She stepped back. He passed her and walked into the public part of her living-room. She closed the door and stood at the end of the sofa, watching him prowl the deep carpet. He stopped to stare at the fireplace. For a crazy moment, she thought he was going to kneel and start tending the fire. She wondered how she could think of this as the *public* area when they had made love just there, lying together on the deep carpet in front of the fire.

'I've been thinking.' His voice was strained. He swung around and they were staring at each other, like two people across a classroom. She had known he would be like this. Frozen. 'We'll get married,' he said coldly, deliberately.

She swallowed. 'Why?' There was no love in his eyes, his voice. She wondered what kind of a marriage it could be.

'Babies need families.' His face was expressionless.

She had to move. She gulped and walked past him, to the fire. She knew it was a warm June day, but she felt the trembling inside herself, like cold. Babies need families. Scott's family had been torn from him at a young age. He was still talking, his words falling into the quiet of her living-room. She tried to concentrate on what he was saying.

'...get married right away. I've got five days before I go back to the Beaufort. It's just long enough. We'll go down to the government agent this afternoon and apply for a licence.'

He dominated the room. He would dominate her life, but when she turned to face him his eyes were flat and lifeless. Not even angry. Whatever had been between them, the warmth and the sharing which had semed strong from the first day—— If she married him with his jaw set and his eyes determined, then it would be gone. He would have locked himself into a trap. A trap of his own choosing, but she would be the gaoler.

She moved her hand, a spasmodic movement. 'You make it sound like getting a fire permit.' Her voice was jerky, too.

Fire. There was no fire in him at all. Not now. He had it all under control. He started pacing, then stopped and stared at her, his hands clasped behind his back. He had worked all this out. What she thought, what she felt, did not matter. She was just a game piece he was moving. He wanted it that way, without feeling.

He said tonelessly, 'You can stay here for the summer. It would be better, until I'm finished my season in the Beaufort, if you were close to your friends. After that, you'll move to Cortes Island.'

'To your house?' It was a plan for strangers. 'Will you give me a room of my own?' He had built walls in his mind to keep her out. Walls. Rooms.

'If that's what you want.' He said the words as if he did not care.

She said abruptly, 'I'm going to make coffee.'

He did not follow her into the kitchen. She should have known he wouldn't. He had not come for intimacy, for sharing. He had come to look after his obligations. She poured water into the reservoir in the coffee-maker, spooned coffee grounds into the filter. She heard the music start. If she married him, it would be like this forever. Scott in the next room. Playing her music, touching her soul. She stared **at** the coffee-maker as it gurgled and hissed, and she thought of the letters in the basement. Charlie, hopelessly in love with Amanda. Her parents, together, walking through the life they had chosen.

She tried to shift her reality, to turn what she was feeling into a poem, words for a song. But it was too real. She could not remove herself from her own feelings by making them poetry.

She brought the coffee to him in the living-room. He was in the private part now, standing at the window, his shoulders broad through the warm brown of the knitted shirt he was wearing. She put the coffee down and felt the barriers in him. She could not reach, could not touch. She curled her fingers inwards, nails digging into her palms. Touching was important to her, she realised. Touching and loving. Better to live without him entirely than to walk through a life of walls and tension.

'Coffee,' she said, and he turned, as if he had not heard her until that instant.

The music was a soft background. Not her love songs, not Robin's deep emotional voice. He had picked a neutral, classical piece. Background, filling the silence. He did not reach for the cup she had set down on the end table for him. They stared at each other for an endless moment.

She clasped her hands together behind her back, licked her lips and whispered, 'Do you love me?'

His jaw flexed. Something in his eyes flared briefly and was gone. She felt tightness in her throat and swallowed.

'Scott, I want a marriage with love, with intimacy. I...I can't marry you if you're doing it just because...because you see it as your duty.' She saw his chest expand, felt the tightness in his breathing.

His words were stilted. 'I assume that it *is* my child?'

She felt as if he had struck with his closed fist. She gasped and his jaw became even more rigid. She blinked and managed to win a victory over the tears that wanted to flow. She whispered, 'I did not get pregnant to trap you. This is not a trap.' But it obviously felt like a trap to him.

Under his hardness must be some emotion, some caring. She had to believe that, had to trust her instincts. Loving Scott was not something that would go away, but if there was ever to be a chance for them, he must acknowledge their love, too.

'I didn't plan to have your baby,' she said, whispering. 'It just—that night . . . it was right. Loving, feeling love for you—— ' His jaw clenched in a spasm, but she remembered what had been in his eyes, in his voice as he whispered against her naked flesh. She said, 'You loved me, too, that night. We made a baby that night, and it will be a child of love. I don't regret it, and I *won't* regret it. I won't have him—I won't have our baby grow up in anything but a home of love.'

If she stayed, he would have to say something, to deny her truth, so she left the room as if she were running. She was afraid that if he denied what they had shared, the denial would become his truth forever.

She went to her music-room. Her haven, she thought uneasily, knowing she could not hide from her world, knowing she should face Scott and say something. But she could not handle it even one minute longer, her heart aching and her voice trembling, the tears so close—and his eyes so cold and closed.

She shut the door. He would not come into this room. If he did, he would be exposing himself to all the things he was afraid to acknowledge. Loving and risking. She did not close the shutters. She could hear the birds outside, and she would hear his truck when he started it. She wanted him to stay, but knew he would leave. He had come to offer marriage, but her price was far higher than he would pay.

Love.

Oh, God! Was she wrong? He had been dragged through homes that did not want him as a child. Maybe he could never reach for her. Maybe she was the one who had to take chances, accept his stilted proposal of marriage and hope he would learn to let himself love her.

She went to the window when she heard the sound of his truck. She watched him drive **aw**ay, almost certain that she had just made a terrible mistake.

By eleven-thirty that night she knew that she had been mindless, asking a man who was afraid to love for words that would commit him. She dashed out and started her van, roaring down the hill and along the highway to the ferry terminal. If she was fast enough, there might be time. His car was probably aboard by now, but she could get a foot passenger ticket and run on just before they pulled out. She saw the lights of the ferry ahead, her hands trembling on the wheel because it wasn't too late yet. The ferry wasn't gone yet.

Then she saw the other lights behind her, red and blue lights flashing. Oh, God! Not *now*! The police. She jerked the wheel and stopped on the shoulder, hoping desperately that the police car would tear on past her, on its way to something more urgent than a mere speeding driver.

But the police car stopped too, pulling up behind her. She watched in her rear-view mirror as the officer got out and walked slowly forward to her car.

'In a hurry?' He looked very young, but his face had the stern authority to back up the uniform.

'I—I have to get to the ferry. It's——'

'Can I see your driver's licence and registration, please?' His voice was politely critical. 'If you'd gone slower, you'd have got there more quickly.'

It was no use. She rummaged in the glove compartment for the registration, in her bag for the driver's licence. He took the documents and went back to his car. She sat, watching the rear-view mirror, knowing it was going to take too long.

The officer came back eventually, after checking on the radio, she supposed, that she wasn't a wanted criminal. He was writing out her speeding ticket as she saw the lights of the ferry moving away from the dock. Too late.

She called Scott's home two days later. There was no answer. She called again the next day and wondered what she would say if he answered. He did not answer and she did not dial his number again.

She called the Caribbean two weeks later. Amanada answered, her voice that magical, husky music that had enchanted her audiences for decades.

'Darling,' she breathed, 'I was just going to call you.'

Melody laughed, knowing it was probably not true. 'How's the act?' she asked. 'Are you still throwing the West Indies on their ears?'

'Of course, darling. What about you? Have you written a gold for Robin yet?'

'Next week,' Melody said. She twisted the cord from the telephone around her index finger. Amanda sounded worried. 'I thought I might come down and catch your act. I could use a holiday.'

'You'd be crazy,' said Amanda repressively. 'Come in the winter. Right now it's a steam bath here. You'd be dripping all over the hotel, and the audience is hell. Honey, it's the off season.'

Melody frowned. 'I want to see you.' To tell them about their coming grandchild, that had been her idea when she picked up the telephone, but Amanda had problems of her own.

Amanda said coolly, 'We're not at our best during the hot season.'

'What's wrong?' Something was. 'Is Charlie OK?'

Amanda did not have a quick answer to that question. Melody demanded urgently, 'He's not sick?' Three years ago he had had a heart bypass. Ever since, he had insisted he was a young man again. Forty at least.

'No. Of course not.' Amanda took a noisy breath, then admitted, 'He's having trouble remembering his lines.'

Melody closed her eyes on a vivid picture of her parents. She did not know which town to attach the memory to. There had been so many. Just another memory, Charlie throwing back his words to Amanda on cue, and the audience laughing. Backstage, hidden in the shadows, Robin and Melody watching. After the laughter, came the hush. The music, and the Connachers had drifted from silence into a soft duet that caught the heart-strings.

'Mom——'

'We've been thinking of retiring,' said Amanda briskly, covering emotion now. Melody thought of Scott, covering emotion. Amanda said, 'I'm the business head, of course. I'm always the one counting pennies.'

'If you need a loan, you can always hit me up,' said Melody, careful to keep her voice light.

Amanda laughed and Melody relaxed. If her mother could still laugh, things would be all right. 'I'll hit Robin,' her mother said. 'I saw him on satellite TV yesterday. That concert in LA, and they mobbed him. They love him. And his new album's a winner. The title song——'

'Where did you hear that? It's not been released yet.'

Amanda laughed, a sound of happy victory. 'We've got our contacts, darling.'

It was the stuff of her childhood. Theatre talk. Melody let Amanda lead them away from the personal. They had never leaned on each other. Affection, yes, but all the Connachers knew how to stand alone. Even she and Robin, supporting each other as children because their parents were often away, but not sharing the secrets of their souls.

'I still thought I'd come down there,' said Melody.

'All right. If you must. Although I'd rather you waited a while.' Amanda paused, then said, 'And think about what you want to do with the house.'

'What?' Melody looked around her. The house. Her home. It had been hers and Robin's since they were teenagers. 'What do you mean?'

'Money,' said Amanda. 'I'm sorry, honey, but if Charlie and I are going to retire, we've got to liquidate some of our assets.'

'This house? You're going to sell *this* house?'

'Well, yes.' Amanda's voice was brisk again now that she had introduced the subject. 'So if you and Robin would get together and think about it. Whether you want it. Because, you see, we've had an offer. You remember Wendy and Ronald Saunderly? Last year, they were up for an autumn holiday. A good offer, and if we accept it, we can walk out on the club here.' She laughed, a sharp sound. 'Rather walk out before we get the axe, you know. Charlie would like to know we quit because *we* decided it was time.'

An offer for Melody's home, the house she and Robin had grown up in, the house she had naturally assumed she would have to bring her baby up in.

'The Saunderlys?' She remembered them. Talkative, too energetic, the woman raving about the peace and quiet as she bustled around the island. 'How long do you and Charlie have to make up your minds?'

'Fourteen days. Well, from the offer date. That was three days ago.'

Three days gone already. If Melody had not called her mother, would Amanda have called her? 'I'll talk to Robin. How much was the offer?'

Melody suppressed a gasp at the answer. From a purely practical point of view, her parents would be crazy to refuse an offer like that. Melody could not hope to match that price unless Robin wanted to share ownership of the house. A house that meant nothing to him, except that it was his sister's home.

Two weeks less three days, but she found herself doing the same thing Amanda had done, putting off calling Robin to talk about it. She hugged herself, wondering what there was in the world that was hers. Everything seemed to be slipping away. Robin's life and hers had been separate for years now, ever since she had left Los Angeles. Her parents would probably never come back to this country to live now. Amanda had said something about buying a place in Mexico. Melody was the only one clinging to the Connacher home on the islands.

She should not feel that a future without this house was a formless unkown. She still had the job at the radio station, and she could build a music-room anywhere, couldn't she?

She did not expect Scott to call. She knew his schedule as if it were her own. He had gone to the Beaufort on the twenty-fourth of June. She had deliberately set herself the task of re-organising her music library that week, and on the Wednesday night she had made sure she was very busy. She should be thinking about Amanda and Charlie, about how much money she could scrape up, and she was, in the back of her mind. In the front was the decision of how many categories to sort her music into, and whether Robin's albums came under the category of pop or easy listening.

She was playing the latest, analysing it, when the telephone rang. She picked it up without even thinking of Scott's name.

'What's been happening?' he asked, casually as if he were an old friend and not the lover she could never forget.

She sank into the big easy chair, cradling the telephone against her shoulder, breathing his name silently. Aloud, she said, 'Not a lot. I talked to Robin yesterday. He and Robbie are moving into the house he bought this week.' *Scott!* Her heart was pounding so hard she could hardly hear him talk.

'I know. I got a letter from him just before I left Cortes Island. He says that the little hernia is virtually gone. And Robbie's teething. And he has Donna's nose, which I wouldn't have guessed myself.'

She smiled, closing her eyes and knowing she could listen forever. They were friends, weren't they? Even if he could not admit to the love, he would not deny their friendship.

He asked, 'What's the music I hear in the background?'

With her eyes closed, she could pretend he was here, in the room with her. 'Robin's new album. It came by registered mail this morning.'

'I'd like to hear it.'

She wished he could be here with her. She could hold out her hand and he would take it, and they would share the music. 'I'll send it to you. How long does it take you to get mail up there?'

'Better save it,' he said. 'I don't have a disc player up here. Just a little tape player.'

'It's a tape,' she said, wanting him to be listening to the music. Several of the songs had been written with Scott in her mind. It was the only way she could say 'I love you'. 'I'll send it to you. Tomorrow.'

'All right. I'll probably have it in about a week.'

If he called next Wednesday, he might have the tape by then. When he listened, would he know it was love-songs for him? 'Where do you call from? Are you just closeted in there with the radio operator, or do they leave you alone?'

'It's a separate little room in the oil rig.' She heard him laugh, then he said, 'They don't broadcast us all over the rig. I guess the call is as private as any long-distance call that gets routed through a satellite. There's probably a few short-wave listeners around the world listening in, but—— Is everything all right? Have you been working?'

Not private enough for talking about the baby, but they could talk about almost anything else. She said, 'Working? A little. I—no, not really. I tried, but I guess I need a holiday from song-writing.'

Their five minutes were over before she could ask him anything about his day. A week. Seven days. She should be counting days until the deadline on the house offer, but instead she was waiting for Wednesday again, sitting beside the telephone for hours, then jerking the receiver up almost as it started ringing.

'Melody?'

She had to take a deep breath, to still her heart. 'Hi.' It sounded breathless and she tried again, 'Hi, Scott. Is it summer up there yet?'

'As close as it gets.' There was a smile in his voice. She closed her eyes and saw it. She pulled her legs up and said, 'Tell me what you did today.'

The ice flow had been heavier than they expected. Two of the big anchors that held the oil rig had become fouled and they had reset them. Routine, he said, and she wanted to know more.

'Five minutes isn't long to explain how we get those anchors down.' She loved his laugh. She was achingly happy that they were still friends. Time, she thought. If he wanted to talk to her, she could wait for years, and there might come the day when he would love her.

She gripped the receiver so tightly that the blood left her fingers, but she made sure her voice was easy and casual. He wanted it light, casual, so that was how it would be. She said, 'We could talk longer if you had a ham radio up there.'

He was smiling, saying, 'I'm not a ham.'

'You could learn,' she said. 'You're always studying new things.' Their time would be up soon. She bit her lip and said, 'I talked to Amanda.'

'Your mother?'

'Yes. She and Charlie are retiring.' She had not intended to tell him, had not wanted him to think she was loading her problems on him. 'She wants them to quit before Charlie gets fired. He's been forgetting his lines lately.'

He was silent for a few seconds, as if trying to tune in on her thoughts. 'Are you going down to see them?'

'I—maybe. Maybe after summer's over. It's deadly hot down there now, and Amanda doesn't really want me to come. I guess she doesn't want family out there, in the audience, seeing Charlie's bad moments.'

By the time summer was over, Melody would be quite obviously pregnant. Already, she could feel the thickening of her waist, the swelling of her breasts. 'Amanda wants to sell this house, so they can swing their retirement.'

'I thought it was your house. Will you buy it?'

'I don't know.' She shifted uneasily. 'For me, they'd put the price as low as they could. The offer they've got—I don't seem to be able to make up my mind.'

Why had she told him that? As if she wanted something from him. That was exactly what she *must* not do.

He said carefully, 'There's lots of room in my house,' and she closed her eyes painfully. Did he want her there? Really want her? 'That big room upstairs—your music equipment could go in there.'

She did not answer.

'Melody?'

In the Beaufort Sea, aboard the oil rig, Scott heard the signal that his time was up. 'Melody? I've got to go. I'll call next week.'

He wondered where she could be next Wednesday. He wondered what she would do, what decisions she would make while he was stuck in the ice fields, unable to reach her.

He should have told her that he loved her, but whenever he thought of saying the words something surged up and choked him. All the memories of other kinds of loving, and losing. All the years telling himself not to be an ass, never to risk himself again, not for anyone.

He tried not to think about it, tried to concentrate on work and make the days pass. Thursday. Friday. Saturday, and the ice maps were still showing a drift towards the rig. The captain of the rig held a conference with Scott and the captain of the smaller supply ship. They were all nervous.

She wanted love. He could not say those words, but he could build a music-room for her, and she might come even without the words. She would be close. When the child came—that scared him most of all. His child. A child needed love and stability. He didn't know if he could give love to anyone, but even in the midst of studying ice maps and worrying about the drift, Melody and her child haunted him.

On Sunday at five in the afternoon, the captain of the rig decided to pull out. Scott had a bad feeling about the whole operation, but the rig was not his ship and he said only, 'John, have you thought about waiting until morning?'

'I'm pulling out now.' John's voice was still sharp from a long argument with the drilling chief. Moving the rig meant capping the drill site and abandoning it. The chief believed intensely that they were about to hit oil, and hit it big.

The rig was anchored with eight Bruce anchors, four at each end. The supply ship and the icebreaker were responsible for slipping anchor for the rig. It was a task that nobody liked. Before they started, Scott checked the latest weatherfax pictures. There was no storm centre around them, but the wind had been brisk and freshening all afternoon. He didn't like the feel of it. If he had found a storm centre on the latest fax, or even a building depression, he would have gone back to John. As it was, he had nothing to base his feeling on.

The supply ship worked on one side of the rig, the icebreaker on the other. Scott was at the bridge of the icebreaker, watching the aft deck where his first mate, Harry, was working with two seamen.

On the deck, Harry, the mate, was pointing, ordering one of the seamen to pick up the buoy that marked the first anchor. Scott pushed the left throttle slightly forward and the right one back, jockeying the ship with the two prop washes. One of the seamen hooked on to the big cable that led from the rig to the anchor, then Harry limped across to control the winching. Scott saw the pennant come over the stern on to the deck. The second seaman hooked on to the pennant and Harry waved a signal to the bridge. Scott pushed both throttles astern, giving slack so the men could release the cable.

He spoke into the microphone hanging over his head. 'John, you can take number one. We've got the anchor here.'

'Roger, Scott. Anchor number one coming in now.'

On board the rig, a big winch started pulling in the anchor cable. The anchor itself was now below the ice-breaker, at the end of the hundred-foot section of pennant. The next step was to bring the seven-ton anchor on board the icebreaker.

From the bridge, Scott could see that Harry was moving clumsily. The mate had injured his leg last spring and refused to go back to the doctor when it kept paining him. Scott watched as Harry stumbled and got in the way of one of the seamen. He had a vision of Harry crushed between seven tons of anchor and the crash rail.

He reached for the loud hailer microphone. 'Harry! Put the winch on hold and come up to the bridge for a minute.'

Harry came up, frowning and complaining. 'Look, Skipper, if we're gonna get those things up, let's get on with it. It's damned cold out there.'

'Ten minutes won't make any difference. You take the con. I'll do the deck work.'

It was unusual, but not outrageous. Harry had his British Home Trade Master's ticket. By this time next year Scott expected that his mate would have his own ship, and Scott knew that he would never be able to live with himself if Harry lost that aching leg in an accident Scott could have prevented.

As Harry had said, it was cold on deck. Scott worked steadily, directing the seamen. The first of the Bruce anchors came over the rollers and hit the deck with a resounding crash. No one flinched. They were all standing safely behind the crash rails, and the deck was made for blows like this. When the anchor came to rest, the men moved out to secure it.

Even with his thermal underwear, his woollen sweater and the big anti-exposure coveralls, Scott felt the cold everywhere as the wind picked up. He lifted his hand to signal Harry. On the bridge, Harry jockeyed the ship towards the second anchor's marker buoy.

Two anchors. Three. The fourth buoy, then the pennant secured to the winch. The last one. Scott signalled the seamen back as the shank of the big steel anchor slid out of the water. As the anchor hit the deck, the ship heaved on an angry wave. The anchor slid a noisy ten feet before the world stilled again. Behind the crash bars, all three men felt the shuddering blow of the anchor's impact.

'Get the lines on it before it moves again!' shouted Scott, and all three men went into action.

Scott was on his way to the winch when he felt the deck moving again. He spun around, knowing he was too late. The big anchor was sliding as if it were skating on an ice-rink. He could hear it, but it was coming incredibly fast for a seven-ton hunk of metal.

'Crash rails!' he screamed, pushing the seaman beside him towards the rails.

Then he dived, and he could feel it like a slow-motion play. Not enough time. The anchor. His own frail body. The crash rails with safety behind them. He knew he was not going to make it before the anchor hit.

He would never see Melody again, never touch her or feel the gasp in her throat, never hear her voice caressing his heart, never have the chance to build a room especially for her music, for her. He had dreamed of it, of leading her upstairs and seeing the pleasure in her eyes. He had dreamed of going outside, chopping wood and feeling her near, knowing she was upstairs, close by.

Little things. Trivial details of one day following another, with Melody close by, close enough to call, to touch, to feel her presence.

Their child. The idea of fatherhood had terrified him even more than the thought of commitment and loving. Now, too late, he realised that he wanted desperately to give it a try.

CHAPTER TEN

THE hospital corridor was cold and brilliant and completely immaculate. Melody had always hated hospitals, hated the thought of illness and waiting for bad news. She had no reason for it, just perhaps the fear of losing people she loved. She had never before spent a night waiting in a hospital waiting-room, not knowing what would come.

She was scared. More alone than she had been in all her life. There was nowhere to hide here, no music-room, no fantasies. Only the shining hospital that did not have the antiseptic smell she had thought was supposed to go with hospitals. And the man on the other side of the room, as silent as she was, waiting for news that did not come.

It was the personnel officer at the oil company who had telephoned Melody. Personnel had received a request to notify Scott Alexander's next-of-kin of an accident, but his recorded next-of-kin was a foster-mother in a home for the elderly. Scott, however, had visited the personnel office only a couple of weeks before.

'He made you beneficiary on everything,' said the brisk, friendly woman. 'His group insurance policy. His registered pension plan. So I thought you were the one to notify.'

'Where is he?' Scott. Seriously hurt. An accident on the icebreaker.

'They're airlifting him to Calgary.' The woman named the hospital and Melody had grabbed for paper and pen.

162

'They took him to Tuktoyaktuk by helicopter. A doctor met him at Tuk, and is accompanying him to Calgary.'

Tuktoyaktuk to Calgary. Three hours from the Northwest Territories port to the modern facilities of Calgary.

He was in Calgary long before Melody could get there. She had to wait for morning and the jet to Vancouver, then another two hours for a connection to Calgary. Then the hospital, and, it seemed, forever without news.

Scott had been taken directly to surgery, hours before Melody arrived. Then, about the time she landed at Calgary airport, he was rushed back into surgery a second time, haemorrhaging.

She had not seen him, would not be able to see him for hours. Critical, the nurse had said, and the doctor was too busy trying to save his life to talk to anyone.

Melody paced from the window that looked out on endless hospital buildings, to the corridor where eventually the surgeon must appear with news for her.

'Look, miss——'

She swung around. Her silent companion, the other man in the room. He stood, tall and lean and limping slightly as he came towards her. His voice was soft, with a precise accent. British, she decided, amazed that part of her mind could still function.

'Sit down,' he said gently, insistently, his voice taking on the faint burr of Scottish ancestors. 'You cannot pace the floor all day like that. Sit down and I'll bring a cup of tea for you.'

Tea. It sounded far better than the foul liquid she had coaxed from the coffee machine earlier. Even the bitter smell of it had made her feel nauseous.

He was gone for ten minutes or so, and came back with two steaming cups. Real cups, not plastic. She accepted the one he handed her, curling her fingers around it. He pulled a paper bag out of his jacket pocket and brought two doughnuts from it.

'Lunch,' he said. 'Of a sort.'

'Thank you.' Doughnuts, and Scott might be dying.

She breathed in warm fumes from the tea, sipped and felt the heat flow slowly down her throat. Soon she would make herself eat one of the doughnuts. She needed the strength. If Scott—*when* Scott got better, he would need someone. She shuddered, knowing that if he had not put her name on his personnel forms, no one would have called her. She might have been feeling uneasy, a sixth sense telling her something was wrong. She would not have known where or what.

The stranger held out the flattened paper bag. She took a doughnut from on top of it. It tasted sugary, too sweet. She chewed for a long time and finally swallowed without gagging and asked, 'Who are you?'

'Harry. The mate from *Jonathan Cartier*. You're the skipper's woman, aren't you?'

She wanted to be his woman, if he would ever let her that close. She said, 'I love him,' and it felt like a release to say it out loud.

He nodded. They fell silent, waiting together.

When Melody could sit no longer, she got up and prowled the little waiting-room. She walked to the window, then to the corridor. No one there. Back to the window again, then past Harry's feet to the corridor. Only a nurse hurrying somewhere else with a swish of rubber-soled shoes. Would they ever come to say Scott was going to be all right?

Soon, Harry would tell her to sit down. She looked at him, but he was staring at the floor between his feet. She sat down beside him, staring at the doorway to the corridor.

'It's my fault,' he said in a low, soft voice. 'I've got this bad leg, and the skipper's been after me to get to the doctors with it. I'm his mate.' She blinked and he said, 'First mate. Next in command after the Master.' She nodded and he explained, 'Yesterday we were bringing up the rig's anchors, and the skipper must have seen me trip on the deck. It's the cold, gets to the damned leg. I've been afraid to go to the doctors, afraid I'd find out it was—well, anyway, skipper put me on the bridge and took my place. That's why he was there when the Bruce cut loose, instead of safe on the bridge where he should have been.'

She hugged herself, trying to understand the strange terms. 'He's your captain, isn't he?' He nodded and she said, 'If he ordered you off the deck, you had to go. He wouldn't blame you, would he?' She wondered if she would ever feel warm again. 'Could you explain to me what happened? I don't know what the Bruce is, and I need to know what happened to him.'

'The Bruce is the kind of anchor we use on the oil rigs in the Beaufort. Here, have the last doughnut and I'll use this bag to show you.'

He drew the icebreaker for her and she found that asking questions and concentrating on the answers was easier than waiting.

A doctor came finally, trailing a mask and wearing tired lines around his eyes. He nodded to Harry and looked at Melody, saying, 'I'm Dr Walton. The nurse says you're waiting for word of Mr Alexander. Are you a relative?'

She licked her lips. She was the mother of his unborn child, the woman who loved him. Was that enough to entitle her to news? She said unsteadily, 'We're getting married,' because if he lived and if the offer was still open she was going to be his wife. She could not bear to spend the rest of her life knowing that if he needed her no one would call and she would not be there.

The doctor rubbed his forehead with his forearm. 'You can't see him yet,' he said flatly.

'Is he——?'

'In the recovery-room. The haemorrhaging has stopped. He'll have a couple of extra seams in the abdominal area, but he'll probably get through the next fifty years.' The doctor half smiled. 'That man of yours is one tough character. I think it's going to be all right. I—hey!'

She could feel the room spinning, then hard hands gripping her. The world steadied and he was glaring at her, frowning.

'I'm sorry. I just——'

'Get some rest,' he said sharply. Then his eyes became more intent and he said, 'You're gravid, aren't you?'

She blinked, pulling back from his steadying hold. 'What?'

He grimaced. 'Sorry. Medical term. Expecting. A child.' Her startled silence must have answered him because he said, 'Don't ask how I can tell. Something about the eyes. My wife says I should be a witch-doctor.' His voice shifted from indulgent to brisk. 'Look, you get out of this place. Check into a hotel, get some sleep. Have a long, relaxing soak in a tub. Then have a good dinner before you come back. Your man might be awake by then.'

She was breathing again, reassured by his matter-of-fact instructions. 'Can I leave the name of my hotel with the nurse?'

'Yes, and we'll call if you're needed. But don't worry. Your sea-captain's going to be fine. He'll be around to see his grandchildren born. You just make sure you get your rest. And regular meals.'

It was Harry who insisted on taking her to a nearby hotel, Harry who called back to the hospital with the telephone number of the hotel and room number, Harry who ordered room service for her and sat with her to make sure she ate it before he left her to sleep.

Amazingly, she did sleep.

He was asleep when she came into his hospital room. She stopped, seeing his face pale and still over the sheets, his arm outside the blanket, strapped to a board, a needle connecting by tube to an intravenous drip.

She could see nothing but his paleness and a frightening array of tubes leading everywhere. She moved closer, not breathing, reaching out to touch the ashen pallor that was his cheek. His eyes opened. She pulled her hand away. She wanted to say something, but no words would come.

He asked, 'Am I dreaming you?' It was hardly a whisper.

She shook her head mutely.

'Good,' he mumbled, and his eyes closed again.

There was a chair against the window. She carried it to the side of the bed, the other side from the tubes. His breathing was slow and steady.

A nurse came in and checked the bag on the intravenous drip, then left again only to return with a new bag of clear liquid. Melody watched the tubing swinging, her eyes tracing it to a needle in Scott's arm.

'What's in that?'

'Glucose,' said the nurse. 'It'll be a few days before he's ready to eat steak.'

She would wait as long as she had to for him to open his eyes again. And she wasn't going to ask for the moon this time. Just to be close by, to share whatever it was he was willing to share.

He groaned and shifted without rolling under the covers. The nurse said quietly to Melody, 'He's going to be uncomfortable for a while. Doctor says his signs are good, so don't worry.'

Eventually, another nurse came and told Melody to leave. Visiting hours were over. She went back to the hotel. She wondered where Harry was, then remembered that he had said something about going back to Tuk. She tried to shake the feeling of time suspended, but the only thing that really mattered was Scott back there in the hospital bed. She turned on the television and found herself watching the news, realising when the announcer said the date that tomorrow was the day Amanda and Charlie had to give their buyer an answer.

Past time for Melody to call Robin.

'Where the devil are you?' demanded her twin. 'Amanda's been burning up the phone lines. You were supposed to call her. About the house.'

The house. It had seemed so important. 'I'm in Calgary. I—quiet, Robin, and listen,' she added sharply as Robin made exasperated noises. 'Scott's been in an accident. He's—they operated and he's going to be all right. He—internal injuries. They were pulling anchor for the oil rig and the weather kicked up. One of the anchors got loose and caught Scott.'

'Are you all right?'

She said, without thinking, 'Yes, now that I know he's going to live.'

On the television, there was a picture of flames shooting up from an apartment building somewhere, then the announcer's mouth moving. Robin said, 'You're in love with him.'

'Yes.' She seemed to be telling that to everyone except Scott himself. She repeated, 'Yes.'

His voice was muted. 'Odd, isn't it? All these years and neither one of us got caught. Then Donna, and he's her brother.'

'Robin——'

He said quietly, 'Don't, Melody.'

'But you haven't forgotten her. It still hurts. You haven't talked about it, but——'

He said intensely, 'I'll never forget her. But it doesn't hurt as much as it did. I've got Robbie, at least. Still, I'm not likely to forget that I'm the one who asked her for more than she could give.'

Melody closed her eyes and saw Scott in her own living-room. 'We'll get married,' he had said. 'Babies need families.' And she had known that he cared for her, even if he could not call it a name like love.

Not enough, she had told him.

It was years since she and Robin had shared the kind of closeness that enabled them to read each other's thoughts, but he said, 'Give him time. I didn't give Donna enough time, enough room. Don't make the mistake I made, Melody.'

She had, but maybe she would have another chance. She had sent Scott away, but he had called. Only one call a week, Harry had said while he was talking about the ship last night. One call a week, and Scott had chosen to call her. And he had put her name on his life insurance. For the child, of course, but it was a link that would grow between them. She remembered how he had cared for his nephew, little Robbie. He had said he didn't know how to be a father, but there had been love in his eyes and his voice as he'd held Robbie.

'I'll try not to,' she promised her twin. 'Will you call Amanda for me? Tell her I don't want the house. You don't want it, do you?'

'No. It's a nice house, but it's my past, not my future.'

Hers, too. Her future was with Scott, whether he was ready to accept it or not. 'Am I dreaming you,' he had asked. As if he expected her to be in his dreams. He had offered her his home, and she would go there. She would let him build her a new music-room, and she would make a home for him there. A family for him.

There was something else she had to do. For her family. 'Robin, Amanda said Charlie's flubbing his lines.'

'Damn! Poor old beggar. So that's why they're talking retirement.'

'Yes. I wanted to go down there, to—well, in case they needed anything from us. And just to go. But Amanda was pretty determined I shouldn't.'

Her twin said, 'I don't doubt it. Charlie would hate to blow his lines with his only daughter there to see him perform.' He thought for a second, then said, 'Look, I'll go down. They haven't met Robbie, and I've got a couple of weeks before the screen test thing Peter's got me lined up for. I'll take the grandchild down, and Charlie will never know he's being watched over.'

'Perfect. And if they ask for me——'

'You're tending the fevered brow of their future son-in-law. Same to be introduced at a later date, and, no, you don't want the theatrical family descending and frightening the poor lad off.'

She choked on a laugh that was half sob. Robin was assuming a lot, and so was she. If Melody looked like moving in on him, Scott might just run hard and fast the other way.

Meanwhile, Scott was getting better, and being far too irritable for Melody to feel tempted to tell him how much she loved him, how her world was moving again because she hadn't lost him to a big anchor and the angry sea. She visited him every day, but daily he seemed more restless and bad-tempered.

The doctor took her aside as she was arriving at the hospital one afternoon, saying, 'Listen, you're the one who's going to have to keep him in line. The fool is determined to ignore the fact that he's not a hundred per cent.'

'He's not worse?' She panicked.

The doctor sighed explosively. 'No. Healing too quickly for his own good. He's getting restless, and I can't stop him from going home. But I've managed to get a pretty good picture of his plans. He expects to be chopping wood next week, and working on some damned building he's got to get done upstairs.' He frowned and said sternly, 'He's got to lay off it for at least six weeks.'

She was not at all sure that she could influence Scott's actions, especially as he grew more impatient and moody with each day of hospital convalescence. Dr Walton was adamant that he must not leave hospital for at least eight days after the surgery.

'And you absolutely have to have someone there to look after you,' he added on the seventh day.

Scott frowned mutinously at that. Melody was standing at the window, looking out and listening. She turned around and said to Dr Walton, 'I'll be there to look after him. I'm going home with him.'

'And no wood-chopping,' went on the doctor. 'No swinging hammers or axes or lifting weights, or whatever nonsense you've got in mind. Not until I've had you back here in four weeks' time to check that incision.'

Scott nodded curtly, his eyes avoiding Melody's.

'All right, then,' said the doctor. 'Tomorrow you're free.' And he walked out.

Melody could hear his shoes squeaking as he went down the corridor outside. A buzzer rang in the corridor. Scott said curtly, 'Who decided that you're coming home with me?'

She crossed her arms and cupped her elbows with her hands. 'I decided. You need someone, and—and——' And she loved him. She flung her hands out and said in an exasperated voice, 'Stop being so difficult. You know you need someone.' She swallowed, gulped and added steadily, 'If you don't want it to be me, then I'll get a nurse.'

'God forbid! I've had it up to here with nurses!'

'Then you're stuck with me, aren't you?'

They stared at each other, both breathing a little heavier than normal. Then Scott made a gesture of impatience. 'Go and get some rest. I'm tired.'

She tried to tell herself that he hated being sick, that so many men were poor patients. Look at Charlie the Christmas she and Robin had turned nine. And Robin with chicken pox. She giggled and thought of her twin at seventeen, laid low by a messy, itchy child's disease. Scott, with his recent foul temper, was in good company.

Theoretically she understood, but she had trouble coping with his bad temper.

He hated being an invalid, so she tried not to be obvious about watching over him the day they went to the airport, but just getting dressed and sitting in the taxi seemed to have exhausted him. He growled at her all the way to the airport, but the first real explosion occurred as they got out of the taxi at the terminal.

'Dr Walton arranged a wheelchair,' she told him. 'Just wait here and I'll collect it.'

He blocked her way, his face pale and his eyes angry. 'I am not going through this terminal in a damned wheelchair like an invalid!'

A porter, rolling past with a cart of luggage, craned his neck to stare.

'You're crazy,' she said, wishing she hadn't chosen exactly those words when she saw the irritation in his

face. 'Scott, who do you think they have wheelchairs for
in an airport? Be sensible and——'

'I don't need it.' He reached for her bag and she jerked
it back.

'No. You're not to lift anything heavy.'

He cursed and walked into the terminal. They walked
to the gate in an angry silence. She could see the muscle
in Scott's jaw twitching from tension as he stood waiting
for his boarding-pass to be accepted by the security agent.
Then he moved stiffly into the waiting-room and took
a chair.

She sank down beside him and heaved a sigh of relief.
He was sitting with his eyes closed, head back against the
wall. He opened his eyes as she watched. They stared at
each other.

'I suppose I'm being totally unbearable?'

Her lips twitched. 'You're not your usual charming
self.'

'Sorry.' He grimaced. 'The wheelchair might have been
an idea. See if you can organise one in Vancouver.'

Then he picked up a magazine from the table beside
him and concentrated on reading it until the pre-boarding
call came. To her relief, Scott made no objection to their
boarding ahead of the others.

He stood back so that she could have the window seat,
then seemed to fall asleep as soon as he sat down. She
wished that she had asked Dr Walton to keep Scott an
extra day or two in hospital, but knew Scott would never
have stood for it.

The plane began to turn slowly, moving away from
the gate. Melody flexed her fingers, tensing for what was
coming. The stewardess moved to the front of the cabin
and the routine instructions began. Melody craned her
head to be sure she had located the emergency doors.

'You're nervous about flying?'

She jumped at Scott's voice. 'I thought you were asleep. I'm not exactly afraid, but I drive when I can.'

Outside, the world started to spin past them in a blur, the jet roaring down the runway in preparation for takeoff. Melody felt Scott's hand cover hers. His felt cool and dry.

'It's all right,' he said quietly.

She realised then that she was pressed back into the seat, her fingers curled into the arms. He turned her hand over and threaded his own fingers through hers. When she looked at him, his eyes were closed again, but he still held her hand.

The jet left the ground with a sickening lurch. A moment later Melody closed her eyes against a glimpse of the wing pointing down at Calgary. She did not open them again until she heard the sound of the engine changing as they levelled off above the clouds.

The first thing she saw was Scott's hand, and her own fingers clenched tightly through his. She relaxed her grip, looked up and found his eyes on her.

'OK now?'

She nodded.

'I'll be here for the landing, too, just in case you want to hang on.' She stared at him and he said seriously, 'I haven't had much practice soothing fears, but I'll do my best.'

She stumbled with an apology. 'I don't mind landings so much. I just tell myself it's almost over, we're almost down, and it's easier. With the take-off—— You know, I always take the ferry when I'm going to LA, with my van. That way I can drive as far as Vancouver, leave it there and fly to LA.'

The stewardess came to Scott's side and he ordered milk for both of them. 'Milk?' Melody echoed. 'I'd have liked a——'

'Milk,' he said firmly, sending the stewardess away with a nod. Then he said quietly, 'You're feeling a bit nauseous, aren't you? The milk might help. I noticed you've gone off coffee lately.'

She had learned that she could avoid most of the morning sickness if she did not drink coffee. She was not comfortable with telling him that, or for that matter with his noticing her discomfort. The baby was a subject she found very difficult to talk about with him, perhaps because she did not really know how he felt about it...or about her.

She was relieved that he slept most of the way to Vancouver. She saw the stewardess about a wheelchair for Scott in Vancouver, and was promised one would be waiting for them when they disembarked.

To her relief, Scott did not object when the time came, although he refused to consider her suggestion that they break their trip in Vancouver and stay overnight in a hotel so he could get some rest.

'I'm not a bloody invalid,' he snapped when she made the suggestion.

'Do you want to get better or not?'

It was a good thing she had not gone in for nursing. She seemed to have no patience at all. They hardly spoke through the rest of the journey. Just one word from Scott. *'No!'* he said, when she suggested another wheelchair at Campbell River.

They came off the plane, into the last terminal. Soon, she thought, she would have him home and then, surely, he would go to bed and get some rest. She did not like the colour of his skin, the deepening lines on his forehead, and she was exhausted herself.

He sank into a seat at the Campbell River terminal and ·e said briskly, 'If you'll just give me your keys,

I'll bring your truck around. It's in the parking lot, isn't it?'

He uttered one short, tired expletive and she snapped back, 'Scott, there's no reason I can't drive your truck!'

He closed his eyes and muttered, 'They're back on the *Jonathan Cartier*. My keys. My wallet.'

It was too much. She had dealt with his temper all day, and now this when she was so close to exhaustion.

'What?' she asked, hearing the echo of his voice.

'Rent a car,' he said, and it was the measure of his own exhaustion that he did not insist on going with her to the car-rental counter.

CHAPTER ELEVEN

MELODY sat on a rock at the water's edge, her legs crossed, her chin in her hand, staring at a place where a loon had disappeared a moment ago. Two weeks, and neither she nor Scott had mentioned the future.

Magical weeks, if she did not think ahead. They had gone for long, slow walks through the lightly populated island. Scott had taught her the names of the trees, the nesting patterns of a multitude of strange seabirds. In return, she had started to teach him Morse code.

From his telephone, while he slept, she had called Laurie at the radio station, apologising for leaving her high and dry.

'I can't tell you when I'll be back. Or if,' she'd admitted. 'You'd better find someone else.'

'Let's leave it in the air,' said Laurie. 'I'll fill in a bit myself. I always miss the hands-on stuff. Let me know.'

The next day Scott took her to a deserted cliff-side where he showed her the bald eagles nesting. She told him about her one disastrous appearance on stage when she was seven years old. She had frozen and Charlie had ad-libbed all around her, and she'd refused ever to go on again.

She made quiche and he ate it, and they laughed about his calling it egg pie, but he refused to eat yoghurt when she bought it. He made a fire in a pit outside and they had a barbecue because he said he'd never been to a barbecue when he was a child.

She wanted to tell him that she loved him, but was afraid to say the words in case he would not want to hear.

He told her about Tom, the foster-father who had taken Scott on his fishing boat and taught him to love the sea. About Sylvia, Tom's widow, who hated being left alone and lived in a home now.

Another day, while he slept, she called Amanda and Charlie and learned that the papers had been signed. The house was sold. She called Mrs Winston and warned her the buyers were coming to look.

'You're moving, then?' said the woman who had been housekeeper to the Connacher twins since their childhood.

'Yes,' said Melody, because that much was certain. Mrs Winston deserved to be told more, but Melody could only say, 'I'll call you when I know something definite.'

Soon, she would have to go home and pack. She put off the decision, put off worrying about where she would be moving. Once, Scott had told her that she could move into his home, that he would make room for her music upstairs. Once, he had said they should marry. But since his accident he had not referred to either the marriage or the unfinished room upstairs.

He talked freely about his other plans for the property on the Gorge. He was going to build a small bathhouse and sauna at the base of the hill behind the house. He wanted to turn the unfinished downstairs room where she was sleeping into a library some day. He drew sketches of his plans and asked for her ideas, but he never said one word that referred to her staying.

She did not have the courage to ask him.

Behind her, she heard the door of the veranda as it swung shut. A few minutes ago the telephone had rung.

Something to do with the machine Scott was hiring to dig out the foundation for the bathhouse. Although he was not allowed to do any work himself, he was managing to organise quite a bit of action by telephone. Soon, she knew, it would be impossible to keep him from working.

Without turning to look, she knew when he was behind her, knew he would be leaning against the big rock with his arms crossed and his eyes narrowed against the power of the sun.

'Did you get them for Monday?' she asked. Everyday questions. She savoured the sweetness of his nearness.

'No. It wasn't the contractor.'

'Oh.' She twisted and found him watching her. Something in his eyes started her heart keeping time in a slow thud. 'What—who was it?'

'Your mother.'

Oh, lord! What on earth had Amanda said? 'Did—did she want me to call her?'

He shrugged. Yes? Or no? She heard the loon calling from the water behind her, but could not turn to look. He said, 'She said to tell you the possession date is the end of August, and can you organise clearing out the house by then?'

She nodded mutely.

'You didn't tell me the house was sold.'

'No.' Because that would bring up the question of where she was going to move, and she was afraid to break the bubble. She pushed her hair back, wished it were long hair and could drop over her face to hide her confusion. He was not pleased to know that she was homeless. 'I—did you tell her I'd call?'

'I didn't get the chance. She said she wanted to meet me, she and Charlie.'

Oh, lord! She knew what was coming. He unfolded his arms and crossed them again. She bit her lip, very much the same as she had at the age of seven, on stage with everyone watching, messing it up and unable to escape.

'She referred to me as your young man.'

'Robin,' she whispered. 'Robin must have said something.' She wished she could flee, but there was nowhere else she would want to be. She loved him. God, she loved him so much that she knew even her songs would dry up if she could not share her life with him.

'Where would Robin get that idea?' he asked.

She shook her head. From her. Because she had told Robin she loved Scott. She saw a glimpse of colour behind Scott's shoulder and she grasped at the distraction. 'There's a car...or a truck. Coming here, I think.'

'Going past,' he said. He did not turn to look.

The sound of the engine faded. She got up from the rock, wondering what came next. Was he trying to find the words to send her away? If he started talking about support payments and medical coverage, she thought she would scream.

She said helplessly, 'It's time for lunch, isn't it?' Lord, why wouldn't he stop looking like that? She was scared.

He did not answer and she could not stand here just waiting. She said uneasily, 'I feel like I'm on display. As if—I'll make some soup, shall I?'

He followed her to the kitchen. She tried to act as if he was not there, to move around with some kind of purpose. She got out a tin of soup and a saucepan. She went into the odds and ends drawer for the tin opener, stood staring at bits of string and a roll of electrical tape, trying to remember what she was looking for.

Tin opener, that was it. She pushed the drawer in and got the right one open. Scott was looming, saying nothing, and she felt as if everything was going to explode.

'You look as scared as I am,' he said quietly.

She dropped the opener. It clattered to the floor. She bent to get it and he said, 'Leave it.'

She whispered, 'What do you want?' Her throat was dry and tight.

A muscle twitched in his jaw. He said, 'You.'

The ring of the telephone broke the silence. They stood locked in silence as the rings continued. His eyes were almost black with some kind of emotion. She licked her lips and caught her bottom lip between her teeth. The telephone gave one last ring and then stopped.

He said, 'I want you to stay here.' There was no feeling in his voice, although his eyes were black and filled with tension. She swallowed and no sound came. He must know that she wanted above everything to stay with him.

His hands were hanging at his sides, fingers hanging down. His face was haggard. 'When I was a kid, when my parents died, Donna and I went to our first foster-home——' He shrugged, showing no emotion although she knew it was there. 'Donna was just a baby, didn't really know what had happened. I didn't settle in very well. They made it plain—lord, I don't even know what their last name was now, I was supposed to call them Mom and Dad, but they made it plain that if it weren't for Donna, they'd send me back where I came from. Wherever that was.' He shrugged uncomfortably. 'I don't like talking about this. The house was—anyway, after a couple of years we were both moved again. The foster-mother was expecting a child of her own, couldn't handle us.'

She wanted to go to him, to put her arms around him, but something in his voice forbade touching. He said, 'I made sure I worked hard enough to be able to stay at the next place, but I was only working for one thing. To have total control of my own life. I didn't want my happiness in anyone else's hands.'

She had not known the details, but she had known it would take time. She would be patient, would not ask for anything he was not willing to share. She would love him, but she would be quiet about it.

He said, 'I went to sea because the sea doesn't ask a man to be anything but what he is. Because I could——' He shrugged away emotions he could not put in words, and said, 'I bought this place for myself, a place no one could kick me out of.' He added flatly, 'I did not build this house to share with anyone else.' He grimaced at his own words and said, 'This was the place where I was safe.'

Was. Until now. She must have made some sound, because his eyes changed. She whispered, 'Then why are you asking me to stay? You don't have to.' Every word hurt as it passed her throat.

She saw his fingers curl in on themselves. He said harshly, 'When that anchor was coming at me, I knew it was the end. A man doesn't lose in a battle with seven tons of steel and survive it. I jumped for the crash rail, trying to get behind it, and I knew I wasn't fast enough. And the only thing I could think of was you.'

She formed the words, 'I love you,' but the words would not come out.

'I wanted to hold you in my arms, to go to sleep feeling you. I wanted to see you when I woke up in the morning.' His eyes closed and his voice deepened. 'I wanted to see our child, to hold it, to watch you holding the baby we made.'

She moved then and her hand found his chest. She could feel his heart hammering against her palm. He said, 'When we made love, I thought you were too dangerous, that I couldn't afford to feel what I was feeling for you, but I couldn't seem to keep away from you. I had to phone you from the rig, and when you didn't answer——'

'I love you.' It was only a whisper, but this time she managed to get the words out, although he did not seem to hear.

His chest was hard, the muscles rigid under her hand. 'When you came here, the first time, I was just beginning to admit to myself that I needed more than one night with you. I wanted you closer, sharing...the whole idea terrified me, but I couldn't seem to push you away in my mind. Upstairs, that morning, when I asked you to stay for a holiday—I was really starting to ask you to move in, to live with me, but I got scared. I'd never had a relationship that mattered with any woman, wasn't sure I could do it, not with the load of hang-ups I'd carried out of my childhood.'

She told him, 'I wanted to say yes. For a holiday, or forever; but I had to tell you about the baby first.' She felt the shudder go through his chest. 'Scott, I wasn't trying to trap you. I—we can take time. We can——'

His hands possessed her arms, his fingers digging in. 'I know I was terrible...brutal to you when you told me you were pregnant, I...I don't know if—— Can you understand, Melody? I just couldn't cope with it. You were putting all these images in my mind, loving and families and babies, and they were the kinds of dreams

I just couldn't believe in, I'd never—I wanted . . . wanted it all so much that it terrified me, so much that I——'

She slid her arms up, around his neck. He was so tight, so tense. She wanted to tell him that it was all right, but did not know how to reassure him.

His hands moved to her back, bringing her close against him. 'There's just never been anybody that mattered in my life who didn't disappear on me—either by dying or by kicking me out.'

'So you had to push me away?' In a crazy way, she understood.

He nodded, staring down at her bleakly. 'When you told me—I—at first I couldn't believe it. I hadn't even considered it might happen. You. And a child. And love. All in my reach. It would have been heaven, except I knew I was afraid to try. Afraid I'd blow it, I guess.' He shook his head, admitted, 'I'm still scared witless. I want you. I want our baby. But I don't know if I can love either of you, or both of you, the way you deserve. I'm not sure I know how.'

'I love you.' He heard her this time. Her voice was strong and her arms were tight around his neck.

'I need you loving me.' He groaned, 'Melody, without you at my side, my world is all black and white. There's no colour.'

He was still frowning and she covered his lips with hers. 'If I can't love you, I'll never be able to write another song, another poem.'

'Oh, God!' He shuddered, then his lips possessed hers, hard, and his arms held her close and tenderly. 'I dreamed of you loving me. What did I do to deserve you?'

He had loved her. She did not say the words because he was not ready, but she knew that words were unnecessary. His arms were holding her and his eyes were loving her. She shivered and felt his body respond and knew that she was home.

She whispered, 'All my life, I wanted a home that was really mine. Moving around all the time, and the crazy scene that was the music world. I tried to pretend I was at home when I went to Queen Charlotte, but——' She swallowed and said raggedly, 'When you came to my door, that was the first time I believed there was something more to loving than the fantasies I spun in my music-room.'

His hands slid under the loose cotton of her blouse, fingers shaping the satiny flesh underneath. She was losing the slender curves that he had once made love to, but his touch was trembling and his voice intense as he murmured, 'I want to pick you up and carry you into my bedroom.'

He felt her body's response to his suggestion and laughed huskily. She warned, 'You'd better not. The doctor would have my head.' His lips possessed hers and she managed only to gasp, 'What about lunch?'

'Loving first,' he growled, and something seemed to catch in his throat.

She pressed her lips against his throat and said softly, 'You don't need to say it.'

He silenced her with a kiss.

She had thought her body would be awkward, but his touch was magic, and when she trembled she could see his eyes flash in response. Then he took her hand, and they were in his room, moving to the big bed. He lay down with her, touched her, and it was more than it had been before. Deeper and more shattering, filled with a long tenderness that brought tears to her eyes.

'Don't cry,' he said, holding her, slowly exploring her lovely softness with his fingertips. 'Please don't cry.'

She moved closer, into his arms, her flesh merging with his, telling him without words that the tears were for feeling, for fullness. For love, not sadness.

'I love you,' he said, and the world went still.

'Was it hard to say?'

He bent over her. 'I've loved you for so long. The words have been inside, trying to get out.'

'I've watched you with Robbie,' she whispered. 'You're going to make a wonderful father.'

'If you're there to help me. You will be, won't you? You're going to marry me?' She saw his face go harsh and cold, but she understood now that it was only a mask.

'Yes.' She returned his kiss, giving herself up to her lover. 'I love you... I've always loved you. Forever.' She would tell him so often, make sure he did not ever forget.

Then he touched her intimately and she gasped and moved closer, returning his caress. He groaned and moved over her and there were no more barriers. They were together, beyond walls or restraints, pleasuring each other almost beyond bearing. She held him close when she felt the powerful build-up to his release, felt the answering pressure inside herself, heard her voice making formless sounds of needing and loving.

He groaned her name, and his love, as he took them both beyond the stars. Then he held her in his arms, closely against his heart, and when their pulses quieted, they slept. Together.

Outside, on the water, the loon bobbed up from the glassy bay, craned his long neck and looked towards the silent house. Overhead, an eagle swooped down from a cloudless sky. In the kitchen, the can opener lay open on the floor, forgotten.

my VALENTINE 1992

Celebrate the most romantic day of the year with
MY VALENTINE 1992—a sexy new collection of four
romantic stories written by our famous Temptation
authors:

> GINA WILKENS
> KRISTINE ROLOFSON
> JOANN ROSS
> VICKI LEWIS THOMPSON

My Valentine 1992—an exquisite escape into a romantic
and sensuous world.

 Harlequin Books®

VAL-92

HARLEQUIN
PROUDLY PRESENTS
A DAZZLING NEW CONCEPT IN ROMANCE FICTION

One small town—twelve terrific love stories

Welcome to Tyler, Wisconsin—a town full of people
you'll enjoy getting to know, memorable friends and
unforgettable lovers, and a long-buried secret that
lurks beneath its serene surface....

JOIN US FOR A YEAR IN THE LIFE OF TYLER

Each book set in Tyler is a self-contained love story;
together, the twelve novels stitch the fabric of a
community.

LOSE YOUR HEART TO TYLER!

The excitement begins in March 1992, with
WHIRLWIND, by Nancy Martin. When lively, brash
Liza Baron arrives home unexpectedly, she moves
into the old family lodge, where the silent and
mysterious Cliff Forrester has been living in seclusion
for years....

WATCH FOR ALL TWELVE BOOKS
OF THE TYLER SERIES
Available wherever Harlequin books are sold

TYLER-G

Back by Popular Demand

Janet Dailey
Americana

A romantic tour of America through fifty favorite Harlequin Presents, each set in a different state researched by Janet and her husband, Bill. A journey of a lifetime in one cherished collection.

In January, don't miss the exciting states featured in:

Title #23 **MINNESOTA**
Giant of Mesabi

#24 **MISSISSIPPI**
A Tradition of Pride

Available wherever Harlequin books are sold.

JD-JAN

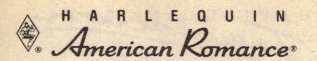

HARLEQUIN
American Romance®

From the Alaskan wilderness to sultry New Orleans . . . from New England seashores to the rugged Rockies . . . American Romance brings you the best of America. And with each trip, you'll find the best in romance.

Each month, American Romance brings you the magic of falling in love with that special American man. Whether an untamed cowboy or a polished executive, he has that sensuality, that special spark sure to capture your heart.

For stories of today, with women just like you and the men they dream about, read American Romance. Four new titles each month.

HARLEQUIN AMERICAN ROMANCE—the love stories you can believe in.

AMERICAN

Rebels & Rogues

All men are not created equal. Some are rough around the edges. Tough-minded but tenderhearted. Incredibly sexy. The tempting fulfillment of every woman's fantasy.

When it's time to fight for what they believe in, to win that special woman, our Rebels and Rogues are heroes at heart.

Josh: He swore never to play the hero . . . unless the price was right.

THE PRIVATE EYE by Jayne Ann Krentz. Temptation #377, January 1992.

Matt: A hard man to forget . . . and an even harder man not to love.

THE HOOD by Carin Rafferty. Temptation #381, February 1992.

At Temptation, 1992 is the Year of Rebels and Rogues. Look for twelve exciting stories about bold and courageous men, one each month. Don't miss upcoming books from your favorite authors, including Candace Schuler, JoAnn Ross and Janice Kaiser.

Available wherever Harlequin books are sold. RR-1

Harlequin Superromance®

Family ties...

SEVENTH HEAVEN
In the introduction to the Osborne family trilogy,
Kate Osborne finds her destiny with Police
Commissioner Donovan Cade.

Available in December

ON CLOUD NINE
Kate's second daughter, Juliet, has old-fashioned
values like her mother's. But those values are tested
when she meets Ross Stafford, a jazz musician,
sometime actor and teaching assistant...and the
object of her younger sister's affections. Can Juliet
only achieve her heart's desire at the cost of her
integrity?

Coming in January

SWINGING ON A STAR
Meridee is Kate's oldest daughter, but very much her
own person. Determined to climb the corporate
ladder, she has never had time for love. But her life is
turned upside down when Zeb Farrell storms into
town determined to eliminate jobs in her company—
her sister's among them! Meridee is prepared to do
battle, but for once she's met her match.

Coming in February
